Rome

Rome

C. N. Phillips

www.urbanbooks.net

Urban Books, LLC
114 Norman Ave.
Amityville, NY 11701

ISBN 13: 978-1-64556-798-1
EBOOK: 978-1-64556-799-8

First Trade Paperback Printing June 2026
Printed in the United States of America

10 9 8 7 6 5 4 3 2 1

Distributed by Kensington Publishing Corp.
Submit Orders to:
Customer Service
400 Hahn Road
Westminster, MD 21157-4627
Phone: 1-800-733-3000
Fax: 1-800-659-2436

The authorized representative in the EU for product safety and compliance
Is eucomply OU, Parnu mnt 139b-14, Apt 123
Tallinn, Berlin 11317, hello@eucompliancepartner.com

To Ryiann, Cahdi, Diamond and Creighton . . . I hope you all know that the stars really aren't that far. Aim for them all. I love you . . . always.

Rome

From The Mind of C. N. Phillips

Part One

Chapter 1

Summer 2000, Atlanta, GA

"Baby, get up. Do you know what time it is?" A woman's voice sounded in a large master bedroom.

Draya Saunders was petite, yet shapely, with a heart-shaped face. Her beauty was that of a timeless classic, and she wore her long hair straight and flowing over her shoulders. It seemed to blow back as she marched to the king-sized bed where a mound lay under the cover. Except it wasn't a mound. It was Rome Johnson. Revered, respected and deadly, Rome was someone many wouldn't dare to cross. However, at that moment, he was simply a kingpin at rest. He stirred in his sleep when the covers were snatched from over his face.

"Ro, get up, baby. Dru's downstairs waiting on you," she said.

Rome finally squinted his eyes open and allowed them to adjust to the light peeking through the curtains in the room. He groaned loudly, clearly annoyed to be woken up, but when he looked at her, his face instantly softened.

"Every time I see you, it feels like the first time," he said earnestly in his deep, husky voice as his eyes examined every part of her.

He was smitten with her doe eyes, button nose, cheek-bones that could land her a magazine cover and her full lips. Rome also loved it when she wore yellow, like the sundress she had on right then. It brought out the golden hue in her brown skin, he always said. Suddenly, he reached for her hand and pulled her down into the bed beside him, surprising her so much that she couldn't help but giggle.

"*Ro,* stop," she was able to say through her giggles as he kissed all over her. "Didn't you hear what I just said? Dru's downstairs, and he been waiting on you."

"If you wanted me up and out of this bed right away, you shouldn't have worn this dress. You know what you was doin'." He took a handful of her big apple bottom and squeezed gently while giving her another kiss.

"As much as I wish we could have a quickie, we can't, baby. Aunt Flo came this morning."

"Damn, I hate that bitch," he said, and she laughed before climbing out of bed.

"I bet you do. I'll tell Dru you'll be down in a minute. Why didn't you tell me Dru got a new car? That thing is gorgeous. I woulda got it in white, though."

Draya left the bedroom and shut the door behind her, leaving Rome lying unsatisfied with stiff morning wood. He groaned again as a sudden rush of regret came over him. He wished he hadn't gotten in so late the night before, so he could have gotten some of the goodness between Draya's legs before she started her menstrual cycle. However, he had to handle some business, and, ironically, blood was involved then too.

Rome forced himself out of bed and went into the massive closet inside the bedroom. He grabbed some shorts along with a red-and-green Gucci shirt to throw on. After a few moments of looking at his large shoe collection, he decided on a pair of Air Jordan 1s. Walking into the en suite bathroom, he flicked on the light and did as he did many mornings. He looked himself over to make sure his humanity was still there. His chiseled chin, thin mustache and his goatee often made him look more serious than he wanted to, but when he showed his perfect, pearly whites, all that seriousness washed away. He ran his hand down his caramel complexion and sighed. Draya often told him that he was too fine to be in the streets, but he never knew what that meant. Finally, as his six-foot-two reflection stared back at him, he focused on his eyes in the mirror before concluding that his humanity was, in fact, still there. In his line of work, there was a thin line between being a human and turning into an animal. Over the years, he'd come across many men who had lost their way due to greed, but Rome had vowed always to move calculated. He loved the money and sometimes had to do unthinkable things to get it. But he never wanted to lose himself to the game because, if he did that, he'd never get out. And the end goal was always an exit. That was the reason there was a beginning in the first place.

Ever since Rome was a kid, he knew he had to be in charge. Not just because he wanted to be; he was a natural-born leader and hustler. He also had a profound understanding that simply possessing those qualities wouldn't make him a boss; he had to apply them. Money had always been the greatest motivator because his household didn't have much of it. His mother, Jelia, was a housekeeper at a local hotel and only brought enough in to make ends meet. And that meant the money ran out after the bills were paid and food was put in the fridge. There was barely any extra for Rome, his younger brother, Dru, or their little sister, Nami. He hated seeing his mother hurting about not being able to provide for them, and even more, he hated seeing his siblings being teased for their tattered clothing. As the oldest, Rome made the executive decision to become the man of the house since their father, Reggie, had run out on them right after Nami was born. He'd started a family with another woman and decided to leave them on the West Side of Atlanta to be with her. Rome always felt that it wouldn't have been so bad had he not moved states and completely forgotten about them. The only thing Reggie left his children with was his blood running through their veins, and, in all actuality, that was all Rome needed to get a foot in the game.

At age 14, Rome approached his dad's baby brother, Charlie, about starting his own operation. Charlie was 35 and, as most would call it, a scrupulous businessman. However, it wasn't a secret in their family where he got all of his money from. And it wasn't from the string of laundromats and clothing stores he owned. Charlie was a drug dealer, one of the biggest in Atlanta at the time. Not only that, but he was also a real killer. Rome smirked, thinking about the conflicted look on Charlie's face when he asked to be put on.

"What the hell you gon' do with a brick of cocaine, Ro?" Charlie had asked him that night in the living room of his luxurious home.

"Shit, if you don't want to front me a brick, front me two pounds of weed, Uncle Charlie. I'll get it off," Rome had confidently answered.

"And I'ma ask you again, what the hell you gon' do with that?"

"Sell it."

"What you need to sell drugs for, Rome? Your daddy did some pussy-ass shit by walkin' out on y'all. That's why I'll never fool with him again, family or not. But you know I got your mama through whatever. She know that. I hate that she never tells me shit."

"Because that ain't your responsibility. I'm the man of the house now. You got in the game when you was my age, right?"

"Times was different back then, though. Shit was easier. Now, you gotta be smart. One wrong move, and you're either dead or locked up."

"You don't think I'm smart? Just because I'm only 14 don't mean I don't know how this shit go. I been around you my whole life, so that mean I been around the game too. So, you gon' front me or what?"

"Your mama would kill me if she knew I got you out here selling weed."

"You ain't gon' have me out here doing shit. I'm my own boss." Rome all but puffed out his chest, making Charlie laugh.

"If I front you, how would you be your own boss?"

"Because when I flip it and pay you back, I'ma re-up. And that would make you my plug, not my boss."

Rome had always wondered if the look Charlie had given him was intrigue or concern. Whatever it was, Charlie agreed to front Rome two pounds of marijuana without asking him exactly how he was going to get it off.

"I don't want your mama knocking on my door, causing a scene," Charlie said in farewell.

"She won't. She gon' be too busy shoppin'."

Some called Rome cocky, to which he always disagreed. He was confident in himself and in his abilities. It might have shocked Charlie when Rome came back in a week with the money he owed, plus enough to buy two more, but it didn't shock Rome. Charlie had some of the best weed in the city, not the dirt other hustlers were pushing. And that meant Rome had it too. It wasn't hard for him to take on all the clientele on his block, which came with some blowback.

"You did what you said you would, and I respect that," Charlie had said when Rome came for his second round of product. "But you can't be out here wide open. Your name been buzzin' in the streets. And you got some motherfuckas real mad right now. You just a kid."

"So?"

"These streets are vicious, Rome, somethin' you gon' learn real fast. I could offer you protection, but I know you got your eyes set on havin' your own shit goin' on. So I'ma give you this instead."

He handed Rome a small black backpack that felt heavy when Rome took it. He unzipped it and looked inside. Not only was the weed inside, but there was also a shiny, chrome pistol and a box of bullets.

"You gon' need that, nephew. These motherfuckas gon' try to do you in, so just make sure you squeeze first. Understand?"

"Fa sho," Rome had said.

Rome's humble beginnings were his favorite tales of his life. Even then, existing in the lavish life he'd created off two fronted pounds of weed, he felt pride thinking about all the hard work and sacrifices it took to move his family out of the hood.

He finished getting ready in the bathroom, but before walking out, he took the black durag on his head off, letting his deep waves breathe. He ran a brush over his hair a few times, and after he was satisfied, he went back into the bedroom to put on the finishing touches for the day—his gold Rolex and gold chain with a diamond "C" pendant on it.

When he finally made it downstairs, he saw his brother, Dru, sitting at the dining room table eating a big sandwich prepared by Rome's housekeeper, Pea. Although

Rome had the kitchen customized for Draya with marble floors, a large marble island, double ovens and white cabinets, it was truly Pea's domain. Rome shook his head at his brother.

"It's morning time. Why the fuck you eatin' a sandwich?" he asked, pointing at the Scooby Doo sandwich.

"'Cause it don't feel like morning when you been up since before the birds chirped, sleepy man," Dru responded in the deep, mellow voice that always got the ladies' attention.

Dru's baby face kept their attention, since he didn't have any facial hair, but he was tall and muscular like Rome. He was a shade lighter than his big brother, like their little sister, Nami. Also, like her, he had acquired the same light brown eyes their mother had, the ones that made their father fall for the woman in the first place. Dru either wore his hair in long, straight back cornrows or an Afro. That day, it was cornrows. He too was wearing a designer shirt and a chain around his neck; however, his pendant was a J for their mother.

"Yeah, whatever. I had a late night last night."

"Late night? You good to check in on Old Lamont's place? DeJuan, Amari and Melo ain't checked in since yesterday morning, and Melo was s'posed to drop that money off to me last night."

His words were a red flag to Rome. Mainly, because Amari, DeJuan and Melo were among his most loyal and had never been late on a drop. He felt his jaw tense, but had to push any negative thoughts from his mind for the moment. Instead, he just nodded.

"Yeah, we gon' go there, but first, we got a cleanup job to do."

Chapter 2

At first, Rome had been against Dru following in his footsteps, especially since, in the beginning, their mother was against Rome bringing drug money into the house. Not because she looked down on it or Rome, but because she didn't want to lose him to the streets or see him behind bars. Rome never wanted that fear to double for her, but although Dru was his little brother, he was his own man. Plus, he was only four years younger than he was, so Rome couldn't stop him from picking up a gun if he tried. And honestly, it felt good to have his own flesh and blood watching his back. It was more motivation to make sure his operation was airtight. Nothing would ever happen to his brother under his leadership.

They rode in Dru's brand-new gold Mercedes-Benz back to the place Rome was the night before. It was an old, run-down warehouse where their Uncle Charlie used to store all his clothing inventory. It hadn't been used in ages, for clothing, anyway. It was outside city limits and a few miles away from any other place of business. Rome always asked Charlie why he wanted a warehouse so far away from everything, and Charlie would always say, "Because it's away from everything."

"Fuck, Ro, is that blood right there?" Dru asked after parking in the empty lot.

He pointed at the front of the building near the entrance door, and sure enough, there was what looked like a bloody hand streak. Rome glared at the spot Dru had pointed out and nodded.

"I ain't mean to leave that there," he said.

"That's too messy. I don't remember the last time you slipped like that," Dru said and shook his head. He let out a long breath. "Do I even wanna know what happened?"

"A motherfucka almost got away from me."

"And what led up to that?"

Rome turned to face his brother with the most serious look that he could muster. The words he was about to speak, he almost couldn't believe them. Before he could even let them out, he had to clench his jaw first.

"We had some snakes in our camp," he said finally.

"Nah," Dru shook his head again, that time in disbelief. "Our shit is too solid. Wouldn't nobody think about crossing you unless they from the other side. And Slaw ain't thought to make a move on you in a while. He been staying in his territory."

"Our shit solid, huh?" Rome chuckled. "I made the mistake of thinking that too—until last night."

Flashback. The night before . . .

"Baby, please make it home on time tonight. I'm tired of being in this big-ass house by myself." Draya's voice came through the flip phone Rome was holding to his ear.

"I'ma try, baby. I just got one more stop to make," Rome answered as he whipped his black Porsche into the parking lot of one of the four warehouses Charlie had left him. "Plus, you not there by yourself. Pea there, ain't she?"

"You mean the lady who doesn't like me? You know, for her to be a Black woman, you'd think she'd be nicer to me. She probably doesn't like me because she thinks I'm stuck-up. And I'm not."

"Well then, maybe you and Pea should try to get to know each other better. She been workin' for us for a year now."

"I'd rather watch TV and wait for you to get here. Hurry up."

Rome smiled to himself when he heard the pout in her voice. Something about her poking out that bottom lip made him fold every time. And if they were making love, it made him come every time.

"A'ight. I'ma see you at home."

They disconnected the call, and he closed the phone. Truth be told, he was already supposed to be on his way home. It was pushing ten o'clock, and he was tired. However, he knew that a shipment had recently arrived from his California connect, and he wanted to check on it. He noticed two trucks parked near him, which wasn't surprising. He figured his soldiers, Clem and Shun, were getting the pack ready to distribute. Out of habit, Rome grabbed the gun from his glove compartment and tucked it in his waist before getting out of the car and walking to the entrance.

The night was still, and the only thing that could be heard was the bugs chirping in the grassy field beside the warehouse. Every warehouse that Charlie had passed down to Rome had been in a remote location, adding more to his boss appeal for Rome. His uncle had always been one of the smartest men he knew.

The enormous metal door groaned slightly when Rome pushed it open. Walking in, the thick air and smell of old dust and fabric hit him immediately like it always did. The lights were on, showcasing a once well used warehouse. It was how Charlie used to traffic all his drugs, through his clothing orders. And now that Rome owned all of his businesses, it became his way of life too. There were remnants of packing tables and clothing all around him, but Rome rarely used that warehouse for anything other than handling his dirty work. He'd chosen that one due to its discreet location and size. Since the shipment at hand was one of his largest orders yet, he was planning something big, something life changing.

In the distance, he could make out Clem, a tall, light-skinned, muscular man, and Shun, a dark, shorter, but still powerful man. The two seemed to be in the middle of having a conversation before Rome entered the warehouse and quickly turned to face him. They were both around his age, at 25, and had been working for him for the last five years. They were young gritters, but they were about their money just like him. However, the closer he got to them, something stood out to him. He didn't see any drugs anywhere—no bags ready to go, nothing still being cut, no pills—nothing.

"What's good, Clem? What's good, Shun?" Rome said with a head nod.

Both returned the gesture. Clem wore his long locs in a ponytail on top of his head and had a mustache that connected to his beard. He had one of those serious-looking faces that rarely changed even when he smiled. Shun had a sweet-looking face, one that looked like he wouldn't hurt a fly. His innocent-seeming demeanor had always made him the perfect hitman. Shun stepped forward and slapped hands with Rome; Clem did the same.

"What up, Ro?" Shun said evenly.

"Y'all straight? Look like y'all was discussing something pretty serious. Everything good with the pack?" Rome asked, looking curiously between the two men.

"Hell yeah. Our bad. We was just talkin' about the distro tomorrow. We wasn't expectin' you tonight."

"Shit, I just came by to see if my boys was good. This a big pack, and I got big plans for it. Speakin' of which," Rome stopped to look around, "where everything at?"

"Already loaded in the back on the truck," Shun said, and Rome nodded.

"Okay, okay." His voice was even.

"Why such a big pack anyway? Somethin' goin' on with Slaw?" Clem asked curiously, and Rome shook his head.

The mention of his opposition's name put a sour taste in Rome's mouth right then, like it always did. The two had been at each other's throats since they were in high school. They had both come up on the West Side of Atlanta and had risen in the drug game. However, Rome had a more dominating presence. He had better drugs, more territory and more foot soldiers ready to do his bidding. As long as Slaw stayed in the territory allotted to him, there would be no problem. But there was always a problem, and that was why the two of them were constantly feuding.

Bodies had been dropped on both sides, and it infuriated Rome because it got in the way of the money. While Rome didn't mind sharing, Slaw wanted the West Side all to himself because Rome had more territory. And Slaw often felt the need to remind Rome that it was only because of his uncle Charlie, to which Rome would respond, "I'm supposed to feel bad for you 'cause wasn't no boss in your family?" When Charlie got out of the game, he left Rome in charge. And he didn't just give him his businesses and territories. He gave Rome all his drug connects too.

"Nah," Rome answered and shook his head. "More drugs just means more money. Faster money. Nobody gotta wait for the re-up."

"We already makin' fast money. A pack this big you gon' have us workin' overtime, and we already workin' overtime," Clem said.

"Pshhh . . . Yeah, man, what's this big plan you talkin' bout? We got a right to know what it is."

"Just know I'm settin' us all up to win," Rome said and began walking toward the back door of the warehouse.

"Where you goin'?"

He heard Clem's voice, but he ignored it and kept walking. He pushed open the door and felt the rush of warm air hit him. The back light on the warehouse lit up the loading zone, and, sure enough, the 14-wheeler truck was there. Rome went over to it, unlatched the door and pushed it up with some force. As he looked inside, he heard the sound of a gun cock behind him.

"I told you we wasn't expectin' you here tonight."

Rome didn't turn around at first. He was too busy looking at the emptiness in the back of the truck, which was probably why he wasn't even surprised to hear Clem's cold voice behind him. Rome took a deep, heavy breath before letting it out and turning around. Sure enough, Clem was standing there, aiming a chrome pistol at Rome's chest. Shun was standing right beside him, looking beside himself.

"Clem, what the fuck you doin'?" Rome asked in an annoyed voice.

"What I shoulda did a long time ago. I'm tired of bein' a runner, dawg. It's time I move up in ranks."

"And you think this is the way to do it?"

"Yeah," Clem chuckled. "Slaw made me an offer I just couldn't turn down. All I gotta do is kill you and deliver your pack to him."

"And then what?" Rome asked, humoring him. "What the fuck he gon' do once the pack runs out? He don't

know my connect. So, after he sells it all, he gon' have to go right back to sellin' that bullshit, and someone else is gon' take over. And that's only if *my brother don't kill you* and *him first. You do know I got cameras in this bitch, right? Did you think this shit through, or you just slow, motherfucka?"*

What he said seemed to leave Clem at a loss for words. Regret flickered in his eyes, and his finger loosened on the trigger. However, that was short lived as anger took full control.

"Man, fuck you, Rome. We out here doin' all this fuckin' work all day, every day, while you move around like a king with yo' bitch," Clem shouted, jerking the gun in Rome's direction.

"That's funny, 'cause my bitch seems to think that I'm always in the streets makin' plays. Because I am. None of this shit moves without me. Clem, you live in a four-bedroom house and just bought your mama a new whip. You think you coulda did that without me and the work I allow you to do? Without me, there's no drugs. Without me, there's no place you can safely move them without gettin' killed. Without me, there's no fuckin' money. And you cross me for Slaw's bitch ass?"

Seeing that the gun didn't intimidate Rome at all made Clem hesitate. Shun looked back and forth between the two men. It was apparent that he too was having second thoughts.

"Aye, Ro, none of this was my idea. I was tellin' him before you walked in that we shouldn't be doin' this shit. I never wanted to betray you. You my boy."

"What? What is you doin'?" Clem asked him with wide eyes.

"You just heard him. He got cameras in the warehouse. You know Dru is just as savage as Ro. I don't wanna be lookin' over my shoulder for the rest of my life behind

you and yo' greed!" Shun looked back at Rome. "I'll go get the pack. It's in our trucks."

He made a move to step away, but suddenly, a loud gunshot rang out, and at the same time, Shun's head snapped to the side. The close range of the bullet made some of his brain particles splash up and hit the ground when his body did. Rome didn't let the shock of Clem killing Shun distract him from the fact that the gun was no longer pointed at him. He pulled his own weapon from his hip and tapped the trigger twice, sending bullets into Clem's shoulder, forcing him to drop his gun, then into his abdomen. Rome kicked the weapon out of Clem's reach and watched humorously as Clem pulled himself back into the warehouse while holding his belly.

"Foolish motherfuckas." Rome chuckled, shaking his head as he slowly stalked behind him. "You had it made."

"Please, man, I got a family," Clem begged in pain as he tried with all his fading might to get away from Rome.

Rome didn't say anything. Mainly because just a few moments before, Clem hadn't even thought about giving him grace. Nor did he think twice about killing Shun, and there was the bigger matter: Rome's drugs were still in his truck. Clem got all the way to the front of the warehouse, where he hoisted himself up on the door and pushed it open with his body weight. Rome let him take one step out of the door, giving him one last feel of fresh air on his skin before snatching him by the collar of his shirt and pulling him back. Clem tried to hold on to the wall outside, causing the blood from his hand to smear when he was yanked into the warehouse. Rome threw him on the ground and glared at him as the gun in his hand hung at his side.

"You know what all this has taught me?" Rome asked, aiming his gun at Clem's head and squeezing the trigger, putting two bullets in his skull. "I gotta tighten up."

***

"Clem and Shun?" Dru asked in disbelief when Rome finished telling him what had happened.

From the expression on his face, Rome could tell that he was genuinely stunned. Had Rome not been the one to go through it, he would have felt the same way. If they could be turned against him, then maybe others in their camp could be too . . . if they hadn't been already.

"I moved the drugs already, but ain't shit gettin' distributed until I know who's with us and who ain't," Rome said.

"So, what's in there?" Dru asked, nodding at the warehouse. "Bodies?"

"What's left of 'em anyway. They bagged up already, ready to go to the farm."

There were many things Rome respected and admired about Charlie, but the main one was that he was the best teacher of the game. He had his hands in many things, more things than Rome knew until he passed them down to Rome. One of those things was a large pig farm in Grayson, Georgia. When Rome had questioned him about why on earth he owned a pig farm, Charlie just laughed.

"Pigs will eat anything until there's nothin' left," he'd said, and Rome didn't need any further details.

Rome made to get out of Dru's car, but Dru grabbed his arm and slightly narrowed his eyes.

"You chopped 'em up, didn't you?"

"How would they fit in this little-ass whip if I didn't?" Rome asked, feeling a small smile come to his face despite the situation.

"Ro, you tryin'a fuck up my interior? We shoulda took *yo'* shit if that's the case."

"Chill, they wrapped up real good. Ain't nothin' gon' leak out. Trust me. Now, let me go. The sooner we handle this, the sooner we can get to the barbershop and see what's goin' on over there."

Dru shook his head in disbelief but reluctantly let his brother get the bodies.

Chapter 3

Nami Johnson did something that morning she often did: show up at her mother's house unannounced. She felt it shouldn't have been a shock since she had only recently moved out. And the only reason she had done that was to have more privacy in her life. Nami was 19 years old and in cosmetology school. Although she was very responsible, that didn't mean she didn't like to have a good time here and there. And dating? Nearly impossible with Detective Nosy in the home. Still, after Rome had set her up with her own apartment, she found herself feeling a little guilty about leaving her mother with an empty nest, which was why she stopped by so often.

Bumping her music loudly, Nami pulled her yellow Jeep Wrangler Sport into her mother's driveway and parked behind her mother's Ford Explorer. She got out and brushed the long, thin, box braids she'd recently installed out of her face. As a very talented hairstylist, Nami liked to be the face of her own brand. Although she was in school to be a cosmetologist, that was just for the license. She already had a long list of clientele she took care of under the table, and braiding was one of her specialties.

She wore a short pink tennis skirt and a white halter top on her petite body, paired with her all-white, shell-toe Adidas. Nami was a beautiful girl with light skin and light brown eyes that could pierce through the soul. Because of what they did in the streets, Rome and Dru were very overly protective of her. They wouldn't think twice about putting someone in a body bag behind her, and she knew that. It was a good thing *and* a bad thing because, sometimes, they were both too overbearing. She didn't know how she would ever have a normal life with them breathing down her neck.

As she walked to the front door of the cute, two-story home, she smiled as she passed the colorful garden. Her mom had always wanted a garden filled with any flower she chose. She claimed that when she was a kid, she had a green thumb, and she proved she'd been telling the truth. Rome had given her the life their no-good daddy never could, and Nami loved him for that. Reaching into her purse, Nami pulled out her house key and tried it in the knob, but to her surprise, it didn't turn. Her face twisted in confusion as she tried it again. However, the same thing happened. Just as she raised her finger to press the doorbell, the door flew open, and she saw her mother, Jelia, standing there wearing purple velour shorts with the matching short-sleeved jacket. She wore a smug look and had her hand on her hip.

"I told your ass I was gonna change that lock if you kept poppin' up over here all the damn time," she said into Nami's shocked face.

"Mama! You changed the locks on me?"

"Hell yeah. You're always poppin' up over here unannounced and shit. What if I had a man over here?"

"Do you?" Nami's interest piqued as she tried to peer over her mom's shoulder.

"Trust me, if I did, I wouldn't have opened the door," Jelia said with a smirk, causing Nami to make a disgusted face.

"Too much information," she said, and Jelia chuckled to herself, stepping aside so her daughter could pass by. "I thought you liked it when I came over."

"I love it when all my babies stop by, but wasn't the point of you movin' out so you could start livin' your own life?"

Jelia led Nami into the dining room where Nami could smell she'd just finished cooking breakfast. There was a plate of eggs, bacon and pancakes on the table in front of Jelia's chair, and she sat in front of it. Nami sat down next to her and reached for a piece of bacon, but to her shock, Jelia swatted her hand away.

"Dang, I can't get no breakfast either?" Nami asked in shock.

"If you wanted breakfast, you shoulda ate before you left that fancy apartment your brother put you in. Or let me guess, you didn't go grocery shopping?"

"I did, but don't nobody cook like you, Mama," Nami said, forcing puppy dog eyes at her mother.

Jelia tried to ignore her daughter, but in the end, she just rolled her eyes and groaned.

"Here, just take it. There's still some more bacon and eggs. I'll just make myself some more pancakes," she said, sliding Nami the whole plate and getting up to start cooking again.

Nami grinned and gladly dug into the plate. It tasted just like sweet heaven. Her mom knew how to make perfect pancakes. She got the edges perfectly crisp every time. She took a few big bites before wiping her mouth, looking across into the kitchen. Her eyes focused on her mother's back as she was over the stove.

"I don't know why you changed the locks, knowing you're just gonna give me a key anyway," she teased.

"No, I'm not. The only one who will have a key is Rome."

"What? Just 'cause he paid for the house?"

"No, because if something happens to me, your brother is the only one who can save me," she said with a wink, and Nami rolled her eyes.

"Is that why he's your golden child? Because he's the only one out of all your kids who has AB-negative blood?"

"No. He's my golden child because your brother knows how to knock. He's the only one out of all y'all that seems to respect the fact that I'm a person and not just y'all mama."

"Damn, I—" Nami stopped abruptly when her mom swiftly turned her head and narrowed her eyes. "I mean, dang. I thought I was doing good by comin' to check on you every day."

"Checkin' on me is fine, baby, but every day is a bit much, don't you think? That's what phones are for."

"Well then, sorry."

Nami's feelings were hurt, and Jelia saw that. She sighed as Nami went from enjoying her breakfast to twirling her fork. She finished making her last pancake and put it on a plate with her other food before going back to sit at the table. Before she started eating, she reached for Nami's hand and squeezed it.

"You know, when the boys moved out, I felt an emptiness that I suppose every mother feels one day. They were so young. Rome was only 17, and Dru was 15. Rome wanted to change our lives, and Dru wanted to protect his brother. I coulda stepped in and stopped it, but I knew I had to let go. I *had* to because no matter how much I yelled or screamed, those streets would always be louder than me. Plus, I still had to raise you. I couldn't be chasing behind them at the same time." Jelia paused and chuckled. "I don't know when the emptiness or the worry went away, knowing what they were doing, but eventually, it did. And I know it's because I let them spread their wings and fly. They proved to me that they were stronger than I thought, strong enough always to fly back home. Rome has kept every promise he ever made to me, and he still has one more to keep, and I know he will."

"What does that have to do with me?"

"Your brothers prepared me for the day I'd eventually have to let you go too. I always knew the time would come when you'd want your own space and your own life. And I want that for you too. I mean, who wants their mama in their business all the time? And you know I'd be *all* up in your business." She raised her brows at Nami in a knowing way, and Nami laughed.

"Oh, I know for sure."

"See? So, don't ever think I don't want you here, baby. But the same way I gotta trust that you're all right, you gotta trust that I am too. Havin' an empty nest is an adjustment, but I'm rediscoverin' who I am as a woman."

"Mama, that's beautiful. I love that for you." Nami smiled and kissed her hand.

"Not as beautiful as you. Now, eat up before you have to go to school."

Nami went back to enjoying her food, and her mom turned on the television in the kitchen. As her mom tuned in, Nami heard the loud sound of a weed eater coming from the backyard. She scrunched her eyebrows together because she had been under the impression that no one else was at the house. She got up from the table to see what the commotion was. The sliding door to the backyard deck was in the large kitchen, so she didn't have to go far.

Peering out, she was expecting to see a gardener of some sort, but instead, she saw a familiar face. It belonged to Jyair Hamilton, one of Rome's soldiers. Although Nami had heard many ghost stories about Jyair, one of them being that he was one of her brother's top shooters, he didn't come off as a bad boy to her. Any time she was around him, he was well mannered and pleasant. She couldn't lie and say he wasn't easy on the eyes, either. His skin was a rich brown tone, like a copper penny, and sweat glistened off his shirtless torso as he moved around in the yard. His mother had a few drops of Puerto Rican blood in her, and that showed in his long, black hair, which was usually pulled back into a braided ponytail. She watched him work magic in her mother's yard for a few more moments before he looked up toward the house, catching her gaze. He smiled up at her and waved, a gesture that she returned before going back to the table.

"Since when did Jyair do your lawn work?" Nami asked as she sat down.

"Ever since Rome started making him come watch over the house every day. I figured if he was gonna be outside, he might as well help me around the house. Now, shhh," Jelia waved her hand frantically to silence her daughter.

She was transfixed by something they were saying on the news, and she used the remote to turn up the volume. Nami had no choice but to pay attention too. They were talking about yet another shooting that had happened in the city. Nami just shook her head.

"Same shit, different day," she said under her breath.

At the same time, the sliding back door opened, and Jyair entered the house, still shirtless. He took off his shoes at the door and came over into the dining room. Nami got a whiff of his sweat and was surprised that he didn't stink. It smelled like a mixture of men's deodorant and expensive cologne.

"Miss Porter, I just got finished with the back. Is there anything else you need me to do for you?"

"No, just get some water, honey, and both of you, please be quiet."

Jyair and Nami exchanged a look, and Jyair grinned. His almond-shaped eyes tilted slightly upward at the outer corners, giving him an intense yet approachable gaze. His nose was well-defined and fit his handsome face perfectly, and his lips were full and inviting. They added a touch of softness to his strong features. Nami just smiled and looked away. He had the kind of smile to give a girl the kind of butterflies she didn't want to feel. Rome would never be okay with her talking to someone like Jyair, even though Jyair was just like him. He walked away to get a water bottle from the fridge, and Nami focused back on the TV. As she watched, she felt a cold chill come over her.

"Is that . . .?"

Her voice faded as she watched the cameraman comb over what had been the scene of a gruesome shoot-out. Yellow tape was everywhere, and officers were still on the scene. They showed a building which Nami recognized immediately.

"Shit!" She heard Jyair say from behind her. "That's Old Lamont's barbershop!"

"Three men lost their lives last night in a deadly shoot-out," the male reporter on the screen said. *"Among them is the owner of a longtime staple in the community, Lamont Brown. Also deceased are Amari Hamilton and DeJaun Couzy. Details on this shooting are still unknown, but we will continue to report as the story unfolds."*

When he was finished speaking, the dining room was silent. Nami knew that "Old Lamont's" barbershop was one of Rome's spots where he did business. She had known Old Lamont since she was a kid. The boys had always gotten their haircuts and line ups from him, and he had always given her candy whenever he saw her. Nami watched her mother's hand go to her mouth in pure shock. She looked over her shoulder at Jyair, the smile long gone from his face. It was replaced with a stony expression.

"Amari . . . dead? They killed my cousin, man. He ain't deserve that shit. I gotta go find Ro!"

"I'm comin' with you," Nami said, jumping up as he went to put on his shoes.

"Like hell you are. You gotta get to class. That ain't got shit to do with you. That's *their* business," her mother said, snatching her arm and stopping her from leaving.

Nami could not resist the helpless feeling that washed over her as she watched Jyair rush out of the house, anguish written on his face.

Chapter 4

"You good, boss?"

The voice, along with all eyes in the room falling on him, interrupted Tyri "Slaw" Wells's long draw of the kush blunt between his fingers. He allowed the high to have its way with him before he looked up and around at everyone who surrounded him. The question had been asked by his longtime shooter, Mac. He resembled a gorilla in both face and stature, making him look menacing without doing a thing. Slaw didn't say anything. Instead, he just passed the blunt before leaning back into the leather couch he was sitting on in one of his decked-out hideouts. Outside of Mac, three other men were in the hideout: Twan, Vonte and Slaw's right-hand man, Bizzy. They'd all been chilling and watching the news on the big-screen TV in the room and listening to them report on a shooting that took place at Old Lamont's spot.

Slaw grabbed the remote from the chair's arm beside him and turned off the TV. He took a deep breath and used his hand to wipe down from his nose to his chin in exasperation. It was apparent he was trying to steady himself before speaking, and the room was silent. Bizzy was the only one who dared to move, and all he did was shake his head.

"The fuck you mean, 'am I good'?" Slaw asked, cutting his eyes toward Mac.

"Slaw, we—"

"Shut up," Slaw cut him off quickly. "Tell me everything that happened last night. Don't leave out one detail."

Mac looked over at Twan, a skinny, bare-faced man who always wore overly baggy clothes and a durag, and Twan looked at Vonte. Out of the three of them, Vonte had always been the trigger-happy one, most likely because he was barely five feet five and always felt he had a point to prove. Vonte rubbed his patchy beard, which looked like it was fighting for its life to grow, and sighed. "A'ight, man, this what happened . . ."

The night before . . .

"Dawg, how much more waitin' we gotta do? We know the pack in there, so let's just go snatch and grab," Vonte's annoyed voice said.

"Nah, we need this shit to be clean. I ain't got time to deal with that motherfucka Slaw. You ever seen him mad?" Twan asked, leaning up from the backseat of the car they were in.

Vonte, Twan and Mac were posted a little ways down from a barbershop called Kool Kutz, owned and operated by someone everyone in the hood called "Old Lamont." Everybody on the West Side of Atlanta knew him, and truth be told, he'd cut all three of their hair when they were coming up. However, when Slaw and Rome started beefing, they stopped going there because it wasn't safe for them anymore. Everyone knew their loyalty was to Slaw, and Rome had most of the West Side on lock.

"Who ain't seen Slaw mad?" Vonte asked like it was a stupid question. "But them boys went in there an hour ago. Who's to say they ain't leave through the back? I ain't tryin'a be out here all night. We already been watching these fools for a month."

It was true that they'd been posted outside for a while, watching the building. However, the blinds had been closed, and they couldn't see what was going on inside. All they knew was that they'd seen Melo, Amari and DeJaun enter like every Friday for the past month, but that time, the three hadn't come back out. Usually, it was a quick process. They went in empty-handed and left with a few heavy-looking bags. No doubt there was money inside.

Since Shaw's men all gotten their hair cut at Old Lamont's place of business, if they had to go in and get what they came for, they knew what the inside of the shop looked like. The front was where the cuts took place, and in the back was an open lounge spot where the barbers took their breaks. Behind that and down a hallway was Old Lamont's office. Although it wasn't a very large establishment, it was big in the community. Not only that, but it was also protected by Rome, which meant if they were caught, there would be hell to pay. They'd have to move swiftly.

"Slaw said to be smooth about this shit," Mac stated. "He ain't tryin'a start a war. He tryin'a send a message to Rome and let him know he ain't untouchable."

"Well, what sends that kinda message like droppin' a body?"

Mac smacked his lips from the backseat.

"Chill the fuck out, hotheaded motherfucka. We all know the only reason you wanna go in there guns blazin' is 'cause DeJaun's pretty-boy ass fucked yo' bitch back in high school."

"Man, fuck DeJaun's black ass. Ain't nobody thinkin' 'bout that kiddy shit or that bitch," Vonte snapped, but couldn't fight off the smirk that came to his face. "I did like that ho, though."

"Stupid ass," Mac laughed.

"Enough of memory lane. What we doin'?" Twan asked. "I hate to say it, but Vonte might be right. What if they went out of the back?"

"They didn't," Mac said.

"How you know?"

"They parked out front, didn't they?" Mac asked and nodded his head to Melo's red Tahoe parked in the distance. "If they parked out front, that means they're leaving through the front."

No sooner had the words left his mouth than the front door of the barbershop opened. They watched Melo step out of the shop. Behind him, Amari and DeJaun exited too, each carrying a large duffel bag. All three men were dressed fly with flashy jewelry and moving cockily, as if they were invincible.

"Now," Mac said, finally giving the okay.

They pulled their black ski masks down over their faces, guns in hand. Under the guise of night, they hopped out of the stolen car they were in and moved quickly to the three men in front of the barbershop. By the time they were noticed, it was too late, as their guns were already aimed at them. All three unsuspecting men looked like deer caught in headlights. Amari went to reach for his waist, but Vonte hit him on the head with the butt of his pistol, causing him to stumble back.

"Drop the fuckin' bags," Vonte's voice boomed as he jerked his gun in Amari's face.

Mac had his gun on Melo, and Twan pointed his at DeJaun. Amari regained his footing, and although he had blood trickling down his face from his short curly Afro, he didn't let the bag go. In fact, he held it tighter. He glared at Vonte with his narrow eyes, not knowing who was behind the mask.

"You know who the fuck you tryin'a rob?" he snarled.

"Yeah, why you think we robbin' 'em?" Vonte responded.

Besides Amari, DeJaun was holding onto his bag too. There were only two options for them to get out of that jam. Give them what they came for, which wasn't going to happen, or fight their way out.

Mac stepped forward and snatched Melo's gun from his hip. When the others tried to take DeJaun's and Amari's weapons, that was the moment they fearlessly lunged at their attackers. Amari quickly pushed the gun in his face to the side just as Vonte pulled the trigger continuously. The bullets missed Amari but went through the barbershop. Amari quickly landed a punch on Vonte's face, making him stumble back that time. DeJaun managed to disarm Twan, and the two of them began tussling as well.

When Mac turned his gun and went to shoot in Amari's and Twan's direction, Melo landed a solid blow on the side of his face. However, even at only 24, Mac was a big man. Melo's punch jerked his face, but his body didn't move. Tired of the games, Mac turned his gun back to Melo and shot him, dropping him to the ground. Then Mac focused his attention back on the others and saw that Amari was on top of Vonte, choking the life out of him. Mac was horrified to see that he had also managed to disarm and pull off Vonte's mask.

"Fuck!" he shouted and ruthlessly shot Amari in the temple, blasting him off Vonte.

Livid that he'd been beaten and unmasked, Vonte grabbed his gun and jumped to his feet before firing multiple shots into DeJuan's back as he was wrestling with Twan over his weapon. But that didn't satisfy his bloodlust. However, suddenly, the door to the barbershop opened again. Old Lamont looked out to see what was going on. He was a taller, older man who had been a sight to see back in his day. His head was bald, but he had a gray mustache and wore his glasses at the tip of his nose. He used to be a spring chicken, but now, his movements are slower. When he saw the three bodies on the ground, he looked at the assailants, his eyes falling on Vonte's face.

"Vonte? Oh no. What the hell are you boys doin' out here? You know Rome is gonna kill you," Old Lamont's upset and reedy voice shouted.

Vonte turned his gun toward Old Lamont and, before anyone stopped him, he fired three shots into the elder man's chest. The bullets hit his fragile body so hard his glasses flew from his face. The life left his old eyes before he hit the ground. Mac stared, stunned at what he'd just witnessed.

"Stupid-ass old man," Vonte said, trying to catch his breath. However, that was interrupted when Mac shoved him so hard that he flew back into Twan. "Yo, what the fuck! You just killed Old Lamont. Fuck! Are you fuckin' stupid?"

"Aye, we gotta go—now," Twan said, and they grabbed the bags.

The three of them ran back to their car, leaving four bodies in their wake.

When Mac got done telling the story, Slaw was eerily silent, and his face was a mask of controlled fury. He stared straight ahead at the three black duffel bags in the chair across from him as Mac's words played in his head. Although he was only 25, Slaw had the demeanor of a man twice his age, which was why everyone had called him an "old soul" since childhood. He was highly respected in his camp . . . or so he thought.

"Didn't I say . . . No one was to harm Old Lamont?" he asked in a low, dangerous tone.

Each word was measured and precise, hardly containing the volcanic eruption simmering beneath the surface. Vonte looked like he wanted to disappear into thin air as all eyes went to him. He swallowed a huge gulp of air when Slaw's gaze found its way to his.

"Slaw, I-I didn't mean to kill him. It all just happened so fast."

"What did? Your fuckin' temper?" Slaw sneered. "Who else saw your face?"

"Nobody. They all dead," Vonte said, and Slaw turned to look at Mac.

"They all dead," Mac confirmed.

Slaw nodded and stood to his feet. He wasn't the type who was into the baggy clothes and sneakers. He liked nice things, and he liked to look like he meant business at all times. He preferred a more fitted look, like the pair of black slacks and silk button-up he wore that day. Around his neck was a gold Cuban link chain, and on his wrist was a gold watch. His late grandfather had told him when he was just a boy that every real man wears a timepiece. Slaw smoothed his hands down his white shirt and walked behind the furniture until he reached the couch, where Vonte was sitting. He stopped when he was directly behind him and leaned down slightly.

"Remind me again what I told you to do."

"Go rob Rome to let him know he could be touched," Vonte said, afraid to look up.

"And how long have we been puttin' this li'l move together?"

"A-about a month."

"A month. So, if I planned a simple robbery for a month, don't you think there was a bigger play in motion?"

"Y-yeah."

"Yes!" Slaw bellowed in his ear, making Vonte jump violently. "Now, we have to prepare for the blowback from your stupid-ass actions! Do you know what you've done by killin' Old Lamont? Huh? *Do you?* A couple of young Black boys dead from gun violence, okay. But a staple in the community? They not gon' just let this go, so that means not only did you kill the one person I told you *not* to, but you also got us hot with the police."

"We got the money, though. Don't that count for somethin'?" Vonte asked quickly.

"*Fuck* the money. It was *never* about the money. It was about throwin' Rome off his game. Now, you ain't did shit but make him wanna go to war."

"I'll make it up, Slaw, man, I swear. I swear I will."

Slaw stood up straight, and feeling his body heat not so close to him, Vonte breathed a quick sigh of relief. What he had done was foolish and stupid. Not only that, but he had also disobeyed a direct order. He wanted another chance to prove himself, but Slaw couldn't have someone who changed the rules as he went in his camp. He couldn't trust him, and he was too much of a liability—to Slaw and everyone else.

"I know you'll make it up . . . with your life."

In one swift motion, Slaw pulled a blade from his pocket and flipped it open. Before anyone had time to react, he plunged it into Vonte's chest. Vonte gasped as the knife pierced his heart. He gasped on what little air was trying to make its way to his lungs, but there was no use if there was no heartbeat. The moment his head fell forward, letting everyone in the room know he was dead, Slaw yanked out the blade and wiped it off on Vonte's shoulder.

"Wrap this motherfucka up and get him out of here before he bleeds out on my furniture," he instructed.

Mac and Twan didn't need to be told twice what to do. They went to one of the closets in the hideout, got some tarp and got to work. As they prepared to dispose of the body, Slaw sat back down in his seat. Bizzy, who hadn't said a word the whole time, passed Slaw the blunt again. The two of them had been best friends for as long as Slaw could remember. Their mothers had been single moms and as close as sisters, raised their boys like brothers, leaning on each other and creating the glue for their children's brotherhood. If Slaw rocked, Bizzy rolled, and that was just how they got down. Although Slaw was the color of peanut butter, he looked light skinned next to Bizzy's chocolate complexion. Slaw preferred a clean-cut look with a low fade and thin sideburns that connected with his mustache and beard. Bizzy couldn't grow facial hair to save his life, but he kept the hair on his head in single twists. Getting women had never been hard for them, but it was funny because women often thought Slaw was the softer one, when really, he was the colder one of the two. Bizzy usually wore a stoic expression. Neither was anyone to play with, though.

"I knew you was gon' kill that motherfucka right after Mac stopped talkin'," Bizzy said in his husky tone.

"Wouldn't you have?" Slaw asked.

"Yeah, I wouldn'ta done it here, though. Ain't you just buy that couch?"

"I'll buy another one," Slaw said and put out the blunt, leaving it in the ashtray. "We got bigger fish to fry."

"What you thinkin'? I mean, the whole purpose of the hit was to get Rome's attention, right?"

"Yeah, but there's an order to action for everything," Slaw said, watching Mac and Twan hoist the tarp they wrapped Vonte's body in and take it out back for transport. "Do me a favor, Biz."

"Anything, bro."

"Make sure our people open their eyes up in the back of their heads. They need to be on point. That stupid motherfucka done prematurely started the war."

Chapter 5

Rome had ignored the constant buzzing of his cell phone until after he and Dru were on their way back to the city. Doing a job like getting rid of murder evidence, he needed to be focused so that he didn't make a single mistake. The last thing he needed was a body to be connected back to him. Rome's cousin, Cynthia, ran the pig farm for him. She was Charlie's daughter, and, as his daughter, nothing surprised her; she was no stranger to crime. She barely gave Rome and Dru a second glance when they got there. Cynthia was a heavyset woman, the kind who found peace away from people. She wanted to leave the city after her divorce and had agreed to live on and run the farm for Rome. The pigs did exactly what Rome knew they would do as soon as the hacked body parts were dropped in their food pen.

"I'll make sure they eat it all, bones and all," Cynthia told them when they were leaving.

He knew she would. It wasn't her first rodeo with him. On the way back, he and Dru stopped at a car wash and thoroughly cleaned out Dru's car, giving extra attention to the trunk. Once that was done, they could officially check on Old Lamont's spot.

"Aye, try Melo's line again. See what's goin' on," Rome told his brother while they were on the highway.

"You don't see me drivin'?" Dru asked, but he still pulled his flip phone out of his pocket. When he looked down, he scrunched his forehead. "Shit."

"What?"

"I got a gang of missed calls from Mama, Nami and Jyair," he said. Rome pulled out his phone as well.

"Shit, me too. I got Jyair lookin' after Mama. Somethin' musta happened." He made to call, but Dru already had his phone to his ear.

"Hello? Mama, you good?" Dru asked. Rome watched his face intensely, hoping that it wasn't anything serious, but the way his brother's eyes widened, he felt his stomach do backflips. "What? No . . . Nah. Can't be."

"What happened?" Rome asked Dru, but he ignored him.

"All right, we like twenty minutes out. Stay home. Jyair left?" Pause. "A'ight. Well, lock all them doors until he get back."

"What happened?" Rome asked urgently once Dru disconnected the call.

Dru once again didn't answer. Instead, he swerved over to the side of the road, putting the car in park. Rome's heart was beating faster than it had in a long time as he watched Dru punch the steering wheel and clench his eyes shut.

"It's Old Lamont . . . They killed him. Mama said it's all over the news."

Time seemed to stop for Rome as Dru's words floated over his head. They couldn't quite land because they didn't make sense to him. Old Lamont . . . killed? When they inevitably landed, Rome felt a rush of every emotion known to man.

"Who?"

"They don't know. Amari and DeJaun was found dead too."

"Fuck," Rome shouted. "Fuck!"

He now understood why Jyair had left. Amari was his cousin. He also understood why Dru hadn't heard from any of them since the morning before. They were dead. And if they were dead, there was only one reason why. The money. He didn't even bother to ask. Rome knew it was gone.

"Who the fuck would kill Old Lamont? Everybody loved him," Rome said more to himself than to Dru.

"I don't know, but we need to get over there, and fast, just in case the money is still there."

"I ain't holdin' out hope for that shit. You don't do that much damage for no reason," Rome said, clenching his jaw as Dru got back on the road. "I'm more concerned about our fallen soldiers. Amari and DeJaun was good people. They was *good* people. DeJaun just had a baby."

Rome closed his eyes and tried not to let fury take over his body. If he didn't compose himself, and soon, the whole city would burn. He was silent the rest of the ride back into the city, memories of Old Lamont flooding his brain. He had given Rome his first haircut and had been the only one who touched his head after that. It was a tough pill to swallow, him being gone. If the news hadn't come from his own mother, he wouldn't have believed it.

Although Old Lamont had his own past in the streets, he never hurt anybody. All he did was cut hair and mind his own business. Rome had a heavy heart and couldn't help but feel like it was his fault. If he hadn't had Old Lamont's barbershop wrapped up in his business, none of that would have happened. Rome never trafficked drugs out of there. However, it was the spot where money was dropped off; that was all Rome used it for. He couldn't even understand how anyone would even know to target it, especially since he changed pickup and drop-off days every month.

When they finally reached the barbershop, everything came full circle for Rome. Seeing the windows shot out and the yellow tape made it real to him. The last of the officers and newscasters were clearing out as they drove by to park. They had been there all morning. Rome noticed the blood on the sidewalk in front of the building. He didn't even know that his jaw was clenching until he felt the tension in his temple.

"Don't blame yourself, Ro. This the shit that happens when people do what we do," Dru said after parking. "This ain't nobody fault but the people who did this."

"And whoever did it, I want 'em dead."

"Once we find 'em, consider 'em bodied," Dru said.

They waited until every cop car was gone before getting out of their vehicle. When they approached the scene, Rome's eagle eyes went to work. They had barely reached the yellow tape when he felt a hand on his right shoulder. He paused, whipping his head, thinking it was a cop, but it wasn't. It was Jyair.

"I been callin' y'all all day. Y'all heard what happened?" he asked.

"Yeah, man." Rome shook his head. "I'm sorry about Amari."

"Thanks," Jyair said in a sad tone that matched the look on his face. "He was one of my best friends. I know his mama goin' crazy right now. I can't be around that energy. Shit too sad. I just wanna figure out who did this shit."

"The police talkin'?" Rome asked.

"Nah, just askin' a bunch of stupid-ass questions. Shit. I can't believe Old Lamont is gone. Who the hell would kill his old ass? He was harmless."

"Somebody without a soul," Rome said, looking wearily at the barbershop.

As he continued to look, something caught his eye. On the side of the barbershop, a young Black officer was motioning to get his attention. "Is that Davis?"

"Yeah, that's him," Dru confirmed. "I think he want us to come over there."

The three of them walked around the crime scene to the side of the building where Davis was. There was no tape over there. When they got close enough, Davis motioned for them to keep following him. They didn't stop until they got to the back of the building.

"What's up, Davis?" Rome greeted him.

"Nothing good. What the fuck happened last night?"

"That's what we tryin'a figure out."

"Killing Old Lamont is crazy. These streets are getting more and more merciless," Davis sighed.

Many would wonder why they were standing there entertaining a cop, but Davis wasn't just any cop. He was on Rome's payroll. He had come up in the same neighborhood as Rome and was about a decade older. He had a wife and a few children to feed. Needless to say, the base salary of being a police officer wasn't cutting it. Rome threw him a few extra dollars every month to be his eyes and ears in the department. He trusted him.

"I agree, but that's how this shit go," Rome said, shaking his head.

"Y'all ain't find anything?" Dru asked, giving Davis a knowing look.

"Money or drugs? Nah. I woulda told you. But I did find something else. I was hoping one of y'all would show up sooner than later. Y'all not too late, though."

"What?"

"Follow me."

Davis took off speed walking to the back door of the barbershop. Rome, Dru and Jyair looked at each other before following behind him. Davis was holding the door for them to walk inside. They stayed on his tail as he went down a hallway toward Old Lamont's office.

"I was the one who responded to the call last night, so I was the first on the scene," Davis explained over his shoulder. "When I got here, I saw the bodies outside, and

Old Lamont's in the entranceway in front. But that's not all I saw."

"What else was there?" Dru asked.

"When I walked in, there were droplets of blood on the marble floor leading back here," he said as they entered Old Lamont's office.

Davis led them over to a wall. It wasn't just a regular wall. It was really a sliding door. There was a room behind it where Rome kept all the week's money. The only ones who knew about it were he, Dru, Old Lamont and whoever was responsible for pickup.

"I cleaned up the blood trail and wrapped his shoulder up the best I could. But he's lost a lot of blood."

"Who you talkin' about?" Jyair asked.

Davis put his hands on the wall and slid it to the side. Rome didn't know what to expect, but when he saw what was in the closet-sized room, relief washed over him.

"Melo!" Jyair exclaimed and dropped to the ground to tend to his friend.

Melo lay there with labored breathing as if he were doing all he could to cling to life. His face was pale, and he had sweat beads on his face and neck. When he heard their voices, his eyes fluttered upward, and he gave them his famous, lopsided smile.

"Took you motherfuckas long enough," he was able to get out.

"I couldn't move him until the others were gone. They would have wanted to question him about what happened, and I know that wouldn't be good for business."

"Yeah, they woulda wanted to know why they was here so late and some more shit," Dru agreed.

"He needs medical attention immediately. It's a wonder how he held out all night 'til now."

"He a survivor, that's how," Rome said.

"I'll go bring my car around back," Jyair said and rushed out of the shop.

Dru went to get Melo some water while they waited for Jyair. When he came back with the small paper cup, Melo scarfed the water down as if he'd never drunk a drop of liquid in his life. Dru went to get him some more since the cups in the shop were so small.

"Ro," Melo panted.

"Save your strength, bruh. I need you to make it out of this shit. We already lost Amari and DeJaun."

At the mention of their names, Rome saw the pain in Melo's eyes. He took a deep breath and tried to blink back his tears. He pursed his lips and shook his head in despair.

"We tried to fight 'em off, but they had the poles on us as soon as we stepped out." He clenched his eyes shut like he was remembering what happened the night before.

"Save your energy, Melo," Rome said again.

"We fucked up . . . but I don't know how. They had to have been watchin' us for a while, or it gotta be a rat somewhere, Ro. We ain't even do pickups at the same time on Fridays. And that's not even the worst part." He looked up at Rome. "I know who's responsible."

"Who?" Rome asked, kneeling to look him in the eyes. "Who did this?"

"Amari was beatin' the fuck out of one of the guys before he got shot, and he pulled his mask off. It was Vonte."

"Vonte?" Rome turned his lip up. "Little-ass Vonte?"

"Yeah," Melo nodded. "It was him and two others. By the build of the one who shot me, that might have been Mac's ass. I don't know about the other one, though."

"But you for sure saw Vonte?"

"Yeah," Melo let his head drop. "My boys gone."

"It's not your fault. All you can do now is heal so you can get back in the field when we go for our get back."

By then, Dru had returned with some more water. He helped Melo drink it until Jyair got there with the car. Then Jyair returned and helped Dru hoist Melo up and out of the hidden room. Rome made a mental note to have someone come clean up Melo's blood once the barbershop wasn't so hot. For the moment, he just closed the sliding door back. When they got outside, he shook Davis's hand.

"Thanks again."

"This is what you pay me to do. I got you," Davis said before walking to where he had parked his car in the back.

Rome went to Jyair's car to make sure they were good for transport. They had to hurry. Rome didn't quite know where Melo was shot, but looking at the dressings Davis had put over his shoulder and chest, blood was still trying to leak out.

"We can't take him to the hospital with a gunshot wound," Dru said.

"Hell nah. The police gon' have too many questions," Jyair agreed.

"We ain't takin' him to the hospital; we takin' him to Aunt Malia," Rome said.

Malia was Charlie's wife. They had been together since high school. She loved Rome and both of his siblings as if they were her own children, and would do anything for them. Malia was a beautiful, educated and well-spoken woman. She had built a successful life for herself. She had never wanted just to be the woman of a rich man. She wanted to be well-off herself, which was why she'd worked and gone to school to become a doctor. After that, she became a surgeon with her own private practice.

"Bet. I'll meet y'all there," Jyair said.

"I'll call her and let her know y'all comin'. Aye? She gon' want you to pull in the back, so her patients don't see him."

"Got you."

Rome watched him drive off, feeling his hand clench into tight fists. He turned to his brother, who was about to head back to where they'd parked. However, the look of fire in Rome's eyes was so powerful that Dru couldn't ignore it.

"What?" he asked.

"When we was in there, Melo told me Amari snatched the mask off one of the shooters while they was fightin'."

"He saw him?"

"Yeah."

"Well, who was it?" Dru asked, and Rome paused. "Who, Ro?"

"He said it was Vonte."

"Little-ass Vonte?" Dru asked just as Rome had.

"That's what Melo said," Rome replied, and a look of understanding was shared between the two brothers.

"You know who he work for, right?" Dru asked just to be sure they were on the same page.

"Yeah. Slaw. And that means Slaw put a hit on us."

"So, what the fuck we gon' do about it? They killed two of ours, plus Old Lamont. We can't let this slide. Slaw just declared war."

"He did . . . So, if it's war he wants, it's war he's gon' get."

Chapter 6

"Mrs. Johnson? Nurse Amanda said your patient in room two is requesting you. She has some questions."

Malia Johnson had just returned to her office to sit down and take a breather for a few moments. Her butt had barely touched her chair when her secretary, Johnna, knocked on her door and poked her head in. Although Malia wanted to let her head fall back and groan into the ceiling, the life she was living was the one she had chosen. She'd always wanted to work in the medical field since she was a little girl, so growing up to be one of the top surgeons in the city was a blessing. Not just that, but opening her own private practice, Johnson's Surgical Care, was what she worked for. However, the news she received that morning was making her move sluggishly around her practice.

"I thought Mrs. Arnold had been discharged already," she said to Johnna.

"I brought her the discharge paperwork, but she didn't leave. She said she has some questions about the surgery."

Malia sighed.

"Okay, I'll be right out."

"And don't worry. After that, your afternoon is free," Johnna said, surprising Malia.

"I thought I had two more appointments today."

"I called and rescheduled them. I heard about what happened to Old Lamont, so I figured you needed some time. I know you were close to him." Johnna gave Malia a sympathetic look.

"I was. Both my husband and I were. Thank you," Malia said with a small, sad smile.

Johnna nodded and closed the door to the office. Once Malia was alone, she blinked back the tears that threatened to fall. Many people had been close to Old Lamont, and she knew many of them felt the way she did then. A part of her wished she hadn't turned on the news that morning, but then again, she would have just found out about his murder in a different way. Malia had met Old Lamont through her husband, Charlie, when they were in high school. She smiled fondly, thinking about the first time Charlie had taken her to the barbershop with him.

"You know you his woman for real if he brings you to the barbershop, right?" Old Lamont had said many years ago.

"And why is that?"

"Any man willing to make all us other men uncomfortable in the shop is a man who's in love. We can't talk about *shit* while you here."

She laughed out loud in her office the same way she had back then. However, this time, the laugh turned into a sob that she stopped immediately. Malia prided herself on being a professional, and she refused to go into Mrs. Arnold's room with puffy eyes or a shaky voice. So, after swallowing the lump in her throat and taking a few moments to compose herself, Malia got up from her desk. Before leaving, she checked herself in the office mirror.

"You'll be all right, Malia," she said to her reflection. "It's gonna be okay."

She straightened the white coat that lay over her pantsuit and fixed some of the curls in her lengthy, natural hair. When she was satisfied with her appearance, she stepped out of her office and maneuvered through the hallway to examination room two. She took a breath and forced a smile on her face before knocking on the door.

"Come in!" she heard the high-pitched voice of Mrs. Arnold.

Malia stepped in and directed her smile to the older woman. Mrs. Arnold was a petite, Black woman in her fifties. She had a cute, puffy face with graying hair she kept straightened, and the strictest eyes Malia had ever seen. Her primary care physician had referred her due to constant complications with gallstones. The next step was to have her gallbladder removed completely, and that was where Malia stepped in. She wanted Mrs. Arnold to feel as comfortable as possible having her as her surgeon, but the truth was, the woman was a little insatiable.

"I was told you have some more questions for me, Mrs. Arnold," Malia said in a kind, patient voice.

"Yes," Mrs. Arnold said, holding up her paperwork. "I see here on this paper that it says, 'less invasive surgery.' What does that mean for me?"

"So, for you, we will be doing laparoscopic gallbladder surgery, which means that the incisions will be smaller and recovery time will be quicker for you than open surgery would be."

"So, I can go right back to work?"

"Oh no," Malia shook her head. "I wouldn't recommend that since you'll still have to undergo general anesthesia and be on pain medication after the surgery."

"Okay. So, how long am I gonna be down? I might be older than you, but I still like to go to work."

"You're going to need to take off one to two weeks, Mrs. Arnold. I don't want you to rush your recovery process. It's okay to rest your body after having a procedure like this done."

"Mm, well, you gonna write me a doctor's note?"

"Of course."

"Good. Mmkay, that's all I wanted to know."

Malia watched as Mrs. Arnold slung her heavy black purse over her shoulder and got off the table. She quickly shuffled out of the room, leaving Malia standing there, shaking her head. A moment later, Nurse Amanda walked in with the hint of a smile on her face.

"That woman is crazy," she said as she began to sanitize the room.

"No, she's not crazy. She's just stuck in her ways and likes things done a certain way, like a lot of people her age."

"I guess you're right," Johnna said. "Are you closing early today?" Nurse Amanda asked.

"Yeah. So, after this room, you can head home. You'll still get paid for your full day."

"Are you feeling fine? You never close this earl—"

"Hold that thought," Malia cut her off, feeling her phone vibrate in the pocket of her coat. She pulled it out and saw that it was her nephew, Rome, calling her. "Actually, I'm going to take this in my office. Enjoy the rest of your day, Amanda."

She excused herself and left the room. When she was out of earshot, she answered and put the phone to her ear.

"Auntie?" Rome said the second he heard her breathe on the phone. "I need you."

"What's going on, Ro? And did you hear about what happened to Old Lamont?" she asked and looked over her shoulder to make sure no one was around as she walked in the hallway. All her staff were minding their own business.

"That's what I'm callin' you about," he said, and she clenched her eyes shut before letting out a heavy breath.

"Please don't tell me you had something to do with that, Ro."

"I didn't. Not on purpose anyway. Some of Slaw's people ran down on mine outside the shop, and Old Lamont got killed in the process."

"Wait, Slaw did this shit?" Malia asked. She finally reached her office and shut the door behind her. She sat down at her desk and tried to process the information. "Slaw is the reason that Old Lamont is dead?"

"Yeah."

"Fuck." Malia hit her hand on her desk. "I shoulda beat his mama's ass back in the day for talking all that shit on my name. But your uncle wouldn't let me because she was pregnant. I coulda saved us a lot of trouble by kicking that demon out of her belly."

"They robbed us too. They got a good hundred thousand."

"How did they even know about any movement through the barbershop? Your uncle never had an issue. You change the pickup days every week?" Rome was silent on the other end. "Hello?"

"I change 'em every month."

"Rome," Malia's voice dripped with disappointment. "Your uncle taught you better than that. Anybody could clock that."

"I know, Auntie. I know. I fucked up, but right now, I need you."

"What's wrong?"

"It's Melo. He was there last night. They shot him and left him for dead. He was able to drag himself into the hidin' spot, but he ain't lookin' too good."

"Where y'all at?"

"On the way to you. Jyair should be pulling up any second."

"Okay, we're closing up early today, so everyone should be about to leave. I'll meet him at the back."

"A'ight. See you soon."

They disconnected the phone, and Malia jumped into action. She didn't know how to feel about Rome's lax behavior being the reason Old Lamont was gone. Mainly because Rome was usually on his p's & q's. She left her office and walked down the hallway to ensure everyone had finished their duties. All the rooms were empty, and when she went to the front, she saw everyone leaving. The only person still lingering was Johnna.

"You aren't leaving?" Malia said.

"I was gonna stay and see if you wanted to go get some food or something to clear your mind," she said.

If Malia weren't in such a rush to get everyone out, Johnna's words would have touched her. But right then, she didn't need any eyes to witness anything that was about to happen. She forced another smile to her lips.

"It's okay, I'm gonna just take care of some paperwork and head home. It's been a long day, and it's only the afternoon."

"You sure? There's that pasta place that you like, not too far from here."

"I'm not really hungry," Malia said quickly. "But maybe tomorrow we can go for lunch?"

"All right, sounds like a plan. See you tomorrow."

Once Johnna packed up her things, Malia walked her to the front entrance and exit door of the practice and let her out. She watched as Johnna walked to her Toyota and waved.

"See you tomorrow," she said, and Johnna waved back.

Once she drove off, Malia shut and locked the door. The next thing she did was go to Johnna's computer and turn off all of the cameras in the building. When she was sure none of them were on, she grabbed a wheelchair and rushed to the back of the building. As soon as she opened the door, she saw and heard a red Mustang skidding to a halt, followed by a gold Mercedes. Dru and Rome hopped out of the Mercedes, rushing over to help Jyair and Melo out of the Mustang. Her heart sank when she saw the state Melo was in. He was pale, and his breathing was shallow, but they were able to get him in the wheelchair.

"He looks bad. I hope the wound didn't get infected. He's been holding on since last night?" she asked as she wheeled him into the building with her nephews and Jyair on her tail.

"Yeah," Rome said.

"Then he's a fighter. I have to get him to the OR immediately," she said. She pointed to the waiting room. "Y'all wait in there so I can try to save his life."

Chapter 7

"They been back there a long time," Dru's voice finally sounded.

It had been a few hours since Melo had gone back into surgery, and they all were sitting on pins and needles. He knew his aunt was doing all she could to save his life, especially since she was a one-woman show. No one had said anything since they arrived. Rome was in his head, and he assumed the others were too. All he was thinking about was how Slaw had infiltrated two of his spots in one night. Rome didn't know how that happened right under his nose. Had he gotten complacent? Was he off his square? Whatever was broken, he needed it to come full circle immediately.

"He alive," Jyair said, breaking the silence.

"How you know?" Dru asked.

"'Cause she woulda came out and said he didn't make it. Plus, God ain't gon' take both my best friends like that. You know what's crazier?"

"What?"

"The only reason DeJaun was there instead of me this week is 'cause Ro asked me to look after Mama Ro. If I woulda been there, I—"

"Woulda been shot up too," Dru said. "Or worse."

Jyair hung his head where he sat, and the sadness and guilt were all over his body. Rome could relate to the blame he felt because he was feeling waves of it himself. Malia had been right to call him out for his poor business practice. He knew he should have been changing the move every week, as his uncle had in the past. But Rome had foolishly thought nobody would be crazy enough to come at him. Especially not at the barbershop. That kind of thinking had now come with three bodies and a possible fourth.

"There gotta be more snakes in our camp," Dru said. "It couldn't have been only Clem and Shun. Even if they knew the drop days, how did they know the spot we was movin' shit out of? And that could mean the other spots aren't safe either."

"Yeah, we gotta switch locations, and for now, only us three can know 'em. And Melo, when he pulls through," Rome added.

"Wait," Jyair lifted his head and put his hands up. "Clem and Shun was snakes?"

"Dead snakes now," Rome told him and filled him in on what had happened the night before at the warehouse.

"Damn, and I always thought they were thorough. I woulda never thought they'd turn on us," Jyair said. "You think they the ones who told Slaw about the barbershop?"

"Nah. I keep shit separate for a reason. Everybody can't know everything. They were in charge of distro. They never knew where the money went. Plus, it seemed like Slaw had *just* got to them. He was tryin'a get the drugs and the money in the same night."

"We gotta have some more slimy motherfuckas around then. Who else know where we keep the money?" Dru asked.

"You, Ro, me, Melo, Dejuan, Amari, Triston and Jax," Jyair listed off the names.

"A'ight, me and Dru will go and press Triston and Jax when we leave here. I need you to go back to my mama's house. I don't trust this motherfucka Slaw. If he cold enough to kill Old Lamont, nobody is off-limits."

"I got you."

The sound of someone clearing their throat got all of their attention. They turned to see Malia standing there wearing blue scrubs and a hair covering. The warm smile on her face confirmed that the surgery was successful.

"He's going to be fine."

"Where is he?" Jyaire asked.

"I have him in a recovery room. Give him a little time to rest, and then he'll be ready to get out of here. You guys can go back and sit with him if you want. Room six on the right."

"Thank you, Auntie," Rome said, relieved.

"Hell yeah. I don't know what we would do without you, for real," Dru said as he and Jyair stood up. He kissed her on the cheek to show his gratitude.

"Probably die," Malia said jokingly, but there was something serious in her undertone. When she saw Rome start to head back, she stopped him. "Wait, come talk to me, nephew."

He let the others go and sat back down in the lobby. Malia sat beside him and turned to face him. For her to want to talk to him, she sure wasn't saying anything. She just looked at him and studied his face until he felt the heat from her gaze.

"What?" he finally asked.

"You know what. What the fuck you got going on out there in them streets?"

"I don't know."

"That's the problem. Your uncle *always* knew what was going on around him. That's how he controlled his environment."

"I know."

"Do you? Because if you did, you'd be moving like it." She cut her eyes at him. "Old Lamont is *dead* because of—"

"Me. Don't you think I know that?"

"No, he's dead because of your lack of attention to detail. Don't you *ever* get comfortable being on top, because there's *always* somebody who wants to trade you out. Do you understand that?"

"I thought I did. Everything been runnin' smooth up 'til now. We ain't had no bodies drop in a while. Not since the last time Slaw tried some foul shit. But that was a long time ago. I thought he knew his place."

"He'll *never* know his place while wanting yours," she said, and her words sent chills throughout his body. When she saw his head drop, she sighed and used a finger to raise it back up by his chin. "Being the leader is more than flipping drugs and making money, baby. It's more than buying extravagant shit and taking care of people. It's about always staying ten steps ahead of everybody else, even the people you trust most. It's about anticipating war so you can stop it in its tracks. It's *everything* because everyone depends on you. Why do you think the head that wears the crown is always so heavy? Your uncle knew."

She let his chin go, and he let her words land how they were supposed to. He was quiet for a few moments, lost in thought. He remembered his uncle would always say, "*Age doesn't make a man a man. Him being willing and able to do the things nobody else can or is willing to do does. That's what makes a leader, and not everybody can be that.*"

"I miss him," Rome finally said, and a sad glint came to Malia's eyes.

"I do too. Every day. But he fought a good fight in life and against that cancer."

Rome turned his head so she wouldn't see the tears that came to the corner of his eyes. Talking about Uncle Charlie's last days always made him emotional. Watching the strongest person he knew slowly deteriorate was harder than watching someone die right away. But before he passed, he taught Rome every single last thing he knew. He never had a son, but Rome and Dru were the closest things he had to one. He'd chosen Rome to pass his torch to, and now, Rome felt like he was failing him. When he gathered himself, he turned back to face Malia.

"What would my uncle have done if he were still here?"

"The first thing he would do is stop blaming himself," she said, raising a brow at him.

"But you blamed me for—"

"My opinion shouldn't matter to you. Learn to silence the room."

"But you my auntie."

"And you the boss, Ro. Don't shit move without you, understand?" she asked, and Rome nodded.

"I understand."

"Good. The next thing he would do is shut down shop to starve out the snakes in his operation. And lastly, he would figure out who killed his people and rip their fucking hearts out. And if he couldn't find them, he'd make them come to him. So what you about to do, Ro?"

Her serious eyes lingered on him as he pondered her words. Finally, his mind settled on an answer, and his gaze matched hers as he spoke.

"I'm about to fuck up the city."

Chapter 8

Rome thought that by the time Old Lamont's funeral rolled around, the weight of his loss wouldn't feel so heavy. But, in fact, it felt heavier. Maybe because he'd gone to the funerals of Amari and DeJaun earlier in the week. Death and final goodbyes seemed to be all that surrounded him. Of course, he covered all costs of their services and put money in their family's pockets as he'd do for any fallen soldier. But when it came to Old Lamont, that didn't feel like enough.

"Although goodbyes are imminent, some we don't see coming in the way they come. But the good Lord makes no mistakes, no matter how they pain our hearts. But . . ." Pastor Knowles's voice wavered, and he stepped back from the pulpit to gather himself. He took a deep breath before stepping back to the mic. "But even I'm shaken and torn by the loss of a soul like Lamont. He might not have come to Sunday service as much as I would have liked, but he was still a dear friend of mine. A good man."

Pastor Knowles had one of those old-school preacher voices: powerful enough to shake a room, and soulful enough to make a person feel his words to the core. Anytime Rome donated to the church, Pastor Knowles would always get on Rome to join the church and walk away from the street life. Of course, Rome would always decline. The most he had to do with the church was writing the monthly check because Pastor Knowles did a lot of good things in the community. It was the least Rome could do since he played a part in poisoning it.

As Pastor Knowles continued, the choir behind him sang in low, harmonious unison, adding to the solemn vibe of the congregation. Old Lamont's funeral service had the church jam-packed with people. Many didn't even have a place to sit, but they were fine standing along the wall as the pastor preached. It was a beautiful, yet sad sight to see. The community cherished old Lamont, and everyone had come to tell him goodbye one last time. The church was filled with low cries and sobs from everyone. Even Rome shed a tear or two.

He and his family were a few rows behind Old Lamont's family, with Draya seated on his left, squeezing his hand. On his right was Dru, and beside him was their mother, sister and aunt Malia. Filling two rows behind them were Jyair, Triston, Jax and many of his solid riders. Rome looked down at the obituary in his hands as the pastor continued to preach, flipping through the short booklet that told a brief tale of Old Lamont's life. There were photos from when he was a baby to adulthood. Rome sniffled when he turned to a page that had a picture of him as a young teen sitting in Old Lamont's chair getting a fade.

"Why he takin' a picture of me like a fuckin' creep?" Rome had asked as Old Lamont finished his cut.

"Aye, watch your mouth while you're in here," Old Lamont had chastised him. *"And he's takin' a picture 'cause I told him to. You're gonna be somebody one day, and that day, I'ma be able to say I gave that boy his very first haircut."*

Rome sniffled as he reminisced. Old Lamont had always believed in him. He felt a sudden heaviness in his heart thinking about the hand he'd played in his death. He felt Draya's hand in his squeeze a little tighter as she leaned into him.

"Chin up, baby," she whispered in his ear. Hearing her voice made him blink away his tears and shift his focus back to the front.

His eyes fell on the open casket and on Old Lamont inside it. The coroner had done a good job at making him look nice, and his family had chosen a tan suit that he would have liked. He looked like he was sleeping and would perhaps sit up at any second.

"I know many of you have stories you'd like to share about your experiences with Old Lamont, and at this time, we welcome you to tell them," Pastor Knowles said.

A line of mourners formed, starting with Old Lamont's children and continuing to his friends. They shared stories of special moments they could recall with the deceased, many of them humorous, which lightened up the room. Soon, the sad occasion turned into a true celebration of life, especially when Old Lamont's best friend of decades got to the podium. His name was Jamison, Jamie for short. He and Old Lamont were thicker than thieves. He was a tall, slender man with balding gray hair.

"Y'all knew this slick motherfucka as 'Old Lamont'—" he started, but the pastor cleared his throat loudly as if to remind him where he was. Jamie cut his eyes at him before turning back to face the congregation. "The Lord knows my heart, and He knows I'ma be the same me whether it be on the streets or in here. Now, like I was saying, y'all knew this slick motherfucka as 'Old Lamont.' I knew him as 'Monty.' I'll never forget the day I met him, back in the day when Lucille's Kitchen was still open." A few of the older people in the church gave satisfied sighs. "Yeah, that was some of the best soul food in the city. We couldn'ta been more than 15 or 16, and well, let's just say he was more into shooting dice and cutting corners than he was into cutting hair at that time. Well, this particular day, he'd gotten into trouble with some local thugs due to some weighted dice he used to beat them outta all their money. I ain't never seen a motherfucka run so fast in my life. He was moving so quick, he didn't even see me come around the corner and ran right into me.

"He dropped the money he was holding in his hands, and I helped him pick it up, but before I could give it back to him, the thugs had caught up to him. There were about four of 'em. They saw that money in my hands and said, 'You in on it too? Let's get 'em.' And you know what Monty did? He stepped in front of me and fought. He coulda kept runnin', but he didn't. And even though I ain't have a thing to do with it, I decided to fight with him. Long story short, that was the first and last time me and Monty met that we got our asses kicked together."

The church rang out in laughter. Rome couldn't hold in his belly laugh. The thought of Old Lamont being young and shooting dice was hilarious to him. Jamie turned to the casket and took a deep, shaky breath before finishing speaking.

"I always wanted to be the one to go first because I knew life just wouldn't be the same without you. I'm gonna miss you, but I'll see you again. Goodbye for now, old friend."

He stepped away from the podium, leaving a lingering effect on everyone in attendance. The church grew very quiet, and no one else moved to speak after him. Pastor Knowles went back to the mic and looked around.

"Does anyone else want to say anything?" he asked.

Slowly, many eyes fell on Rome, including his family's and the pastor's. Pastor Knowles gave him an encouraging nod, and it was then that he looked around and noticed the attention on him. Maybe it was the guilt he felt, but Rome hadn't planned on speaking at the funeral.

"Go head, baby," his mother urged him.

Finally, after a few more seconds, Rome let Draya's hand go and stood up, moving past her. He smoothed down his black suit as he walked up to the podium, feeling everyone's eyes follow him. He usually wasn't a nervous person, and even then, it wasn't the large congregation that made him feel that way; it was the pressure of knowing that his words would be his final goodbye. Rome turned to face the large crowd, many of whom he recognized and many he didn't. He cleared his throat and lifted the mic so everyone could hear him.

"I'ma keep this brief, but what I'll say is it feels good to know how much love Old Lamont had in the city 'cause he deserved it. The truth is, he was a friend, a brother, an uncle and a father figure to many of us. If it wasn't for his guidance while we sat in his chair, many of us would be lost. His shop was more than a barbershop. Yeah, you went there to transform how you looked, but Old Lamont had a way of makin' you change how you think. I know he did that for me." Rome paused as his eyes fell on his aunt, who gave him a slight nod. He looked over at the casket, and a small smile came to his face. "It's not gon' be the same without him here, and I'm not gon' pretend it will ever be. I'ma miss you, Old Lamont. We *all* gon' miss you."

He stepped back, and Pastor Knowles gave him a comforting pat on his back. Rome went back to his seat and sat through the rest of the service, trying to keep his emotions in check. When it was over, the choir sang one more song as the pallbearers carried the casket down the aisle and out of the church, followed by family and friends. Rome and Draya walked together until they got outside, where the sun's warmth hit them. It had been an early service, and it was still morning. Rome didn't plan to go to the repast, but he knew his mom, sister, and auntie could hold it down. Draya hugged him and kissed him on his chin.

"That was nice what you said up there. You okay?" she asked, her eyes dripping with concern.

"As good as I'll be today. You ready to go? We can probably stop and grab some breakfast before I take you home."

"Yeah, let me go say goodbye to your mom and aunt real quick," she said and left him standing there.

But he wasn't alone for long before Dru, Jyair and Melo approached him. Melo's arm was in a sling, and he winced sometimes when he moved, but he was up and alive. Although the funeral service had just concluded, his work never did. Rome gave them all a serious look.

"Have everybody who wasn't at the funeral meet us at the spot," Rome told Dru. "I want Jax and Triston there too."

"Business continuin' as usual?" Dru asked, and Rome shook his head.

"We'll see," Rome replied.

He'd taken his aunt's advice and halted all street sales after the murders in an attempt to draw out the snakes. See, to him, a snake wasn't loyal to anyone, not even the one that fed it, because if it got hungry enough, it would turn on them too.

"Yo, who the fuck is that?" Jyair asked and pointed in the distance.

Nobody else seemed to be paying attention to the black car that had just turned onto the street the church was on. When it turned, it should have picked up speed to keep on going, but instead, it began to creep. The hairs on the back of Rome's neck raised when the windows rolled down, and he recognized the driver of the car as Mac. They seemed to spot each other out at the same time, but whereas Rome would have had to draw his gun, Mac's was already out of the window. He and his goons began blasting gunshots in Rome's direction, and it sounded like the Fourth of July. Dru tackled Rome to the ground just in time, and they hit the pavement hard. A sea of screams filled the air as panic broke loose. Everyone scurried like rats. From where Rome lay, he saw Jyair and Melo firing back at the car. There was a loud screech as Mac hit the gas and sped out fast.

"Fuck, I missed him!" Jyair said, jerking his gun in anger.

"Get up, Ro, we gotta go," Dru said, getting to his feet and pulling Rome with him.

Rome's eyes frantically scoured the crowd of badly shaken people in search of his family. There were only a few unlucky casualties bleeding on the sidewalk, but that was still too many. Rome's thumping heart drowned out the miserable sobs as fear threatened to take hold of him. Finally, his eyes fell on his mom, Nami, Auntie and Draya. They had all taken cover behind the hearse and were huddled together. But somehow seeing them alive didn't ease his spirit one bit. It just made him furious. That was too close a call.

"You seen who that was?" he asked Dru through clenched teeth.

"Yeah, that fat bitch, Mac."

"That mean Slaw's callin' out hits in broad daylight," Melo said, breathing heavily. "What you tryin'a get on? We can go after him."

"Nah, that's too hot. The police gon' be here any second. We need to get ghost," Jyair stated and looked at Rome, who seemed frozen in time. "Rome? You hear me. We need to go!"

Rome clenched his fists and turned his angry gaze to his brother. He was like a dragon, and if fire could come through his nostrils, it would. Slaw had been hitting him back-to-back, and Rome had yet to retaliate. It was no longer a threat of war anymore. It had officially started.

"This motherfucka done killed Old Lamont, and now he sends some hitters to get at me direct? Fuck it," Rome bellowed. "Get *everybody* to the spot—*now*. We at war."

Chapter 9

The morning breeze stroked Slaw's face as he walked confidently through a park toward a bench. Although it was early, and it had rained the night before, people were still out on their morning jogs or walking their dogs. As he walked, his phone vibrated in his pocket. He quickly answered when he saw who was calling.

"Did you get him?" he asked instead of saying "hello."

"Hell nah," Mac's voice came from the other end of the line. "There were too many bodies out there. We shoulda waited 'til shit cleared out some. But we'll get him next time."

Mac had been tasked with the job of trying to kill Rome at Old Lamont's funeral. It was rare for Slaw to have Rome's exact location, so he wanted to take advantage. Slaw would have loved for Mac to call him to say they would be holding Rome's funeral soon, but he knew Rome was just like him . . . a survivor.

"Aim shoulda been better. Go to your spot. I'll pull up on you after this meeting," Slaw said and disconnected the call.

When he reached the bench, he sat down and glanced at his wristwatch. The time read 9:59, and the second the minute changed to 10:00, he felt another presence sit beside him.

"Wade . . . Punctual as always," Slaw said before looking up at the man who had sat there.

Dressed casually in jeans, a T-shirt and shades was Officer Jason Wade. He was a good fifteen years Slaw's senior and had been on his payroll for some time. He was Slaw's eyes and ears in the department and had helped him get out of more trouble than Slaw probably even knew. Slaw was interested in knowing what the cops had to say about the incident at the barbershop, so he called a meeting with Wade.

"You've really outdone yourself this time. What the fuck kind of shit do you and your boys have going on?" Wade asked.

"I just need to know what they know and what they're doin' about it."

"They were able to place your boy DeVonte Moss at the scene of the crime. Named him as one of the shooters."

"And how the hell did they do that?" Slaw asked.

"There's a witness says they saw him plain as day because his mask came off during the murders. You might wanna tell him to lie low because they're looking for him."

That was news to Slaw, especially since he had been told no one else had seen them commit the crime that night. He was visibly annoyed by that revelation, but he took a steady breath.

"You don't have to worry about them finding Vonte. He's gone," Slaw told him.

"Like gone, gone?" Wade asked, raising a brow, and Slaw nodded. "Good. But this still might bring some heat to your door. There's a detective who really has a hard-on for you and Rome."

"Who's the detective?"

"Name's Detective Bradshaw. Younger guy tryin'a make a name for himself by taking down a kingpin. If he can't bring both you and Rome down, he'll settle for one. And right now, you're the only fuckup. And this witness says they not only saw Vonte, who is a known member of your crew, but they also saw the vehicle they drove away in."

"You know who the witness is?"

"No. They're being real tight-lipped about it. They know there are moles in the department on both sides."

"Well, I don't pay you *not* to know shit. Find out. I don't need nobody runnin' their fuckin' mouth."

Wade nodded as Slaw stood up from the bench and walked away from him, going back the way he'd come. As he walked, Bizzy, who had been posted and watched by a nearby tree, joined him on the sidewalk.

"I don't know why you trust that cracka man. He could turn on us any second."

"As long as I keep his pockets lined with dough, he ain't gon' do nothin' of the sort. Also, a dog will never bite a hand if it has more dirt on it."

"I feel you. What he say, though?"

"Just reminded me how much of a stupid-ass motherfucka Vonte was. There *was* a witness, and they saw his face."

"That shouldn't matter though since he dead, right?" Bizzy asked.

"The cops can link him to me, which means the crime can be too," Slaw said, shaking his head. "Wade said the witness saw the getaway car too."

"Who the fuck is the witness?"

"He don't know. They bein' hush-hush about it. But Wade gon' find out who it is. In the meantime, let's go figure out what Mac did with the car."

They reached the parking lot and got inside Bizzy's SUV before heading to Kent's Corner Store. Mac was often posted there, and Slaw instantly spotted him standing outside the store when they arrived. He was in some sort of disagreement with an older woman everyone had come to know as LuLu. She was an addict with a natural slouch in her back and a thirst in her eyes that a drug dealer could spot from a mile away. As usual, she was dressed in mismatched clothing for the wrong season. Her gray hair was disheveled and in a lopsided ponytail. Mac was in the middle of yanking his arm away from her when Bizzy parked the vehicle, and he and Slaw got out.

"I told you already I don't got shit for you, LuLu. Fuck outta here," Mac told her harshly.

"Come on, Mac. I'm hurtin' real bad. Please. Just a small rock, please? I'm good for it. Everybody knows I'm good for it."

"Like I said, I don't got shit for you. I don't even know what you talkin' 'bout."

By that time, LuLu spotted Slaw and Bizzy approaching them, and she turned her attention toward them. Her begging eyes fell on Slaw, scanning him hungrily, waving some crumpled-up dollars in the air.

"Slaw, tell ya boy to serve me so I can get on about my day. I just need a little something to hold me over. I'm hurtin' all over."

Slaw's eyes went from her to Mac. If Mac wouldn't serve her, there had to be a good reason why. He loved money so much that he would take a baby's last dollar if they tried to give it to him. Instead of telling Mac to give her what she needed, Slaw waved her off.

"Damn, Slaw, you gon' do me like that?" LuLu asked.

"Yeah, he is. So, like I said, get ya swerve ass to steppin'. Don't come back over here no more," Mac told her.

"You know what? Fuck all y'all. I need to go find Erica anyway." LuLu glared at them all before she finally turned and scurried off. As she did, she called them every name in the book and flicked them off a few times. Mac just shook his head.

"Swerve-ass bitch," he said.

"Man, that's just LuLu," Bizzy said humorously. "You know she bat-shit crazy."

"Bat-shit crazy, and I think she workin' with them people. Bitch might have a wire on," Mac said.

"LuLu?" Bizzy asked, laughing out loud.

"Man, listen, somethin' been off about her lately. She went from needin' fronts all the time to suddenly havin' the dough to fund her habit. I don't know, but somethin' seem off about that. I told all my boys to stop servin' her. Anyway, what's with the pull up? Everything straight?"

"It will be once you tell me you did the right thing with the car from the other night," Slaw said.

"You know I did what I had to do with that shit. Especially after Vonte did that hot-ass shit," Mac said, but Slaw still wasn't completely satisfied.

"I need to know details," he pressed.

"We bleach bombed that bitch and dropped it off at the junkyard. I watched it get crushed myself. We good," Mac said, and when Slaw's eyes bore into him, he gave him an earnest expression. "We *good,* boss."

"A'ight. 'Cause there was a witness from that night who says they saw the whole shootin'."

"Bullshit. Wasn't nobody out there but us and the dead. I ain't see nobody."

"Clearly, there was somebody else, and I need you to find out who. If they talkin' to the police, they're talkin' in the streets too."

"Word. I'm on it," Mac said and slapped hands with Slaw and Bizzy before the two men walked away.

Before getting back into the SUV, Slaw found himself looking in the direction LuLu had gone. He saw her standing alone at the corner, carrying on a whole conversation with herself. After a few moments, she started walking down the street. He didn't realize how long he'd been staring in her direction until he heard Bizzy clear his throat. He looked over and saw his friend giving him a strange look.

"Where we headed to next?" Bizzy asked.

"We still need to count the money from the job we did to prepare for a re-up. But first, follow that bitch." Slaw nodded toward LuLu.

"You can't be serious? That motherfucka Mac don't know what he talkin' about. LuLu just a harmless swerve."

"Best-case scenario, she's just a harmless swerve. Worst case is that Mac was right. We won't know until we take a look, right?"

"A'ight, man, you the boss," Bizzy shrugged, and the two of them got into the vehicle.

When they pulled away from the corner store, they eased on down the street. LuLu had already made it all the way down the street and rounded a corner. By the time they caught up, she was entering an apartment complex with other addicts loitering around outside. Bizzy parked across the street, but not directly in front of the building, careful not to be too noticeable. Nothing about the scene seemed off-putting to Slaw. It looked like the kind of place LuLu would live. He rolled down his window and motioned for one of the fiends to approach them. He was an older man with a full gray top and beard. He was missing six of his front top teeth, and in his hand, he carried a beer. When he saw Slaw motion to him from the nice SUV, he hurried over. He reeked of malt liquor and cigarettes and smelled like he hadn't had a bath in days.

"Can I help you?" he slurred as his eyes curiously darted all around the inside of the vehicle.

"Eyes on me," Slaw directed, and the man obliged. "You know who I am?"

"Hell yeah. You Slaw. Everybody 'round here know who you are."

"What's your name?"

"Billy."

"Well, Billy, I got a question for you about one of your friends."

"Which one?" Billy asked, glancing over his shoulder briefly before looking back at Slaw. "Is it Lawrence? That's a grimy motherfucka right there. He owe me ten dollars."

"Nah, not Lawrence. You see that woman who passed you a little while ago and went inside the building?"

"Who, LuLu?"

"Yeah. I need to know what apartment she lives in. Can you do that?" Slaw asked, and Billy pondered the request.

"What's in it for me?"

"Some change," Slaw said and pulled out a fifty-dollar bill from his pocket. Billy's eyes lit up, and he instantly reached for the money. But right before his fingertips could touch the bill, Slaw pulled it away. "Apartment number first."

"Shit. Since you wanna be a wise ass and hold the money hostage, I guess I'll tell you the truth."

"And that is?"

Billy looked around him before leaning in closer to the window and speaking. "That bitch don't live here at all. We be tryin'a figure out why she comes here every day, but none of us have an answer."

"Does she know someone who lives here?" Slaw asked, and Billy shook his head.

"I live here, and I ain't never seen her go inside any apartment. She just walks in the front and leaves through the back. I don't know where she goes after that. Crazy bitch. All she gotta do is walk around the building for all that."

"You ever see her with anybody?"

"No," Billy said at first, but then he shook his head as if just remembering something. "Now that I think about it, Lu don't be with nobody at all."

Slaw and Bizzy exchanged glances before Slaw handed Billy the money. Billy happily took it and held it up to the sky to check for the watermark. When he was sure it was a legit bill, he folded it and put it in one of his dingy pockets.

"Thank you, Billy. That's all I needed to know."

Chapter 10

When Rome ensured the women in his life were safe and sound at his home in the suburbs, he and Dru met the others in his operation at his main hideout. He was sure word of the drive-by had spread like wildfire, so it shouldn't have been any shock to them that he wanted to meet. Rome and Dru were still in their funeral attire, although Rome had loosened his tie after all the commotion. As he drove to the hideout, he couldn't read his brother's face. It was set on one setting: blank.

"You good?" he finally asked, but his question seemed to upset Dru. "Aye, I said, you good?"

Dru still said nothing. Instead, he clenched his jaw and looked out the window. By the vein popping out of his temple, it was apparent that his temper was flaring, and he was trying to get control of it. Rome was going to drop it, but then Dru balled his fists and punched the glove compartment in front of him.

"They been hittin' us left and right! And we ain't sent one shot back," he said loudly with his nose flaring.

"Because shit is too hot right now. It's steps I gotta take to—"

"Bullshit! We look weak. We down four men, two of which was gon' turn on us and two Slaw snatched from us. *And* they just popped at us!"

"You don't think I know that?" Rome felt himself growing agitated toward his brother's clear animosity.

"The fuck are we gon' do about it? Plus, ain't nobody makin' no money 'cause you ain't distributed shit. You holdin' a meetin' when we should be in the field gettin' our get back!"

"If I don't know who on our side is fake, why the fuck would I call a play and risk bein' set up?"

"So, what we gon' do then?"

"Trust me."

"I've *been* trustin' you. I'll *always* trust you. But I'ma say what we all thinkin'," Dru said and looked over at his brother.

"Oh yeah? And what's that?" Rome asked.

"We need that old Ro back. The one who ain't give a fuck about makin' it home because he *knew* he was—no matter how nasty it got in the streets."

Dru stopped talking and settled into his seat. Although he was quiet, his voice seemed to linger in the car and in Rome's mind. When they finally arrived at the house, many cars were already parked there. Rome parked his vehicle in front and got out with Dru following. They walked up the sidewalk to the front door, and when Rome tried the doorknob, it was locked. That was how he liked it. He did the code knock that only he and his boys knew. Seconds later, the door swung open, revealing Jyair on the other side.

"Took y'all long enough," he said, dapping Rome and Dru after letting them pass.

"I had to make sure the family was good," Rome told him.

"I should be there. You payin' me to be."

"You good for right now. Pea is lookin' after 'em and cookin' 'em some food," Rome said. "Everybody here?"

"Yeah, in the livin' room," Jyair said.

Rome led them through the hallway and past the kitchen of the fully furnished hideout. Although it looked like a bachelor's pad, it was used for business and business only. And that meant no women were allowed in or out. On any given day, $250,000 or more would be inside, not to mention drugs and many weapons. Rome's rules were ironclad. It wasn't a whorehouse. Their manly urges would have to be satisfied on their own time and in their own homes.

They reached the well-lit living room, and, sure enough, the room was filled with what he hoped were still his most loyal soldiers. When they first entered, there had been many conversations going on at once, but upon Rome's arrival, everyone grew quiet. Of course, Melo was there. He was seated with Triston and Jax on a couch along the wall. Rome noticed his boys, Abram and Leon, to the side at the pool table, in the middle of a game. They were the ones missing in action at Old Lamont's funeral, and seeing them doing something as relaxing as shooting pool was eyebrow raising to Rome. Jyair and Dru went and stood against a wall while Rome surveyed the room. All of them had been with him for years, some since he first came into the game. He searched for a lie in their eyes but found nothing but respect.

"Y'all know why I called y'all here, right?" he started, and they nodded.

"These streets gettin' ugly again," Leon said.

He was a short, stubby man, and although only a few years older than Rome, he'd already started to go bald. Leon was one of Rome's top earners, someone who usually kept the others on track. He'd always seemed content with his place in the operation, and he'd never shown signs of wanting to advance. But then again, one could never be too sure. Rome looked apprehensively from Leon to Abram, trying to read their eyes. Well, Abram only had one good eye, given the fact that he'd gotten shot in the face years before and lost it. He had always been a flashy guy since Rome knew him in high school. The person who shot him was after the expensive watch he was wearing that day. Little did he know he wouldn't be leaving with the watch *or* his life. Abram was as cutthroat as they came, and even when injured, he could come out a victor. He was a very fair-skinned man with thick, red hair and a red beard. He usually wore a patch over his bad eye, and that day was no different.

"Where the fuck was y'all at today?" Rome asked, looking from Leon to Abram. "You too good to say one last goodbye to a real one or somethin'?"

"Nah," Abram sighed and put down the pool stick he was holding. "It ain't nothin' like that. It's just shit. After Amari and DeJaun's funerals? I'm just tired of seeing my people in caskets. I'm a man, but that takes a toll on you."

"Hell yeah," Leon sighed and shook his head. "I been knowing Old Lamont since I was knee high. I ain't want my last memory of him to be laid out like that. I ain't mean no offense to you, Ro."

Rome didn't sense that they were lying, and when he looked over at Dru, his brother nodded, showing he believed them too.

"What we need to be figurin' out is how the fuck they knew to hit the barbershop in the first place. Who been talkin'?" Jax said, looking around.

He and Triston were twins. They both had dark skin and wore their hair cut low. They had the same fashion sense, often wearing jeans with jerseys or nice T-shirts. They would be impossible to tell apart if it weren't for the scar on Jax's cheek that he'd gotten when they were kids. Jax also was the no-nonsense brother with a short temper, while Triston was more easygoing. Jax glared around the room with distrustful eyes.

"Let's not start accusing each other," Triston, a college-educated man, said.

"Then who we gon' accuse?" Jax asked, looking around. "There was already two snakes amongst us. Are there more? Me, you, Melo, Amari, DeJaun, Ro and Dru the only ones who knew about that spot, and I know for damn sure I ain't run off at the mouth."

"I didn't either. And I trust everybody I have running for me," said Triston.

"I trust everybody under me too. They hungry, but none of them would turn on us. Slaw don't even have enough motion to tempt them," Melo chimed in. "And even with that bein' said, I couldn't see Slaw wastin' his time with them. He wants Ro and his operation. That's why he went for Clem and Shun. They had access to the drugs *and* money. So, if it's a snake still among us, they in this room right now. We the closest to Ro and got the most pull in the operation."

Everyone looked around at each other suspiciously. Although Rome called the meeting to get down to the bottom of what was going on, it was then that he realized that wasn't the way he wanted to go about it. And starving his operation wasn't the way to make his enemy come to him. He thought about what Aunt Malia had said and finally sighed.

"Maybe it ain't none of us," he finally said, and everyone turned to face him.

"How can you be so sure if Clem and Shun did that bullshit?"

"I can't be sure. The only thing I'ma tell y'all is you all have my trust until you don't. And the last ones that crossed me? Ain't even no bodies for no funerals," Rome said as his voice turned icy. "From now on, pick up and drop off days will change every week, and so will the location. Whoever's in charge at that time will be completely responsible for my money, which means if some funny shit happens after switchin' up the routine? That's yo' ass. No questions, no excuses. Understand?"

Everyone nodded.

"This mean we get our distro then?" Jax asked. "My customers been fiendin'. It's dry out there. I see why Slaw's ass is mad. They would rather wait on Ro to open shop again than go to him."

"And that's why we gotta tighten up heavily," Dru spoke finally. "Can't nothin' else get through the cracks."

"Agreed," Rome said. "Y'all will have your shit tonight. Get your people ready to work overtime."

"Shit, they're already ready, homie. Let's just get it," Jax said and stepped up and dapped Rome up.

Rome left the room so they could get their game plans together. As he walked out of the house, only one thing was on his mind. Blood. When he reached his car, he heard someone else exit the hideout, and when he looked over his shoulder, he expected to see Dru since they'd come together. However, it wasn't just Dru. Melo and Jyair accompanied him.

"What's next, Ro?" Dru asked, recognizing the bloodlust on his brother's face.

"You said you wanted the old Ro back, right?" Rome almost growled. "Well, I want my fuckin' money back. Or some souls in its place."

Chapter 11

Jelia, Nami and Draya were still visibly shaken by the events outside the church. Nobody had said more than two words to one another. They hadn't been in the home for more than an hour, and the silence was deafening around the dining room table where they sat. Jelia was sipping some wine to calm her nerves, but every so often, she let out a long breath of air. All of their eyes kept catching one another's, showing that they wanted to talk about the morning's events, but no words came out. Rome's housekeeper, Pea, busied herself fixing them plates of Cajun cabbage and corn bread. After the shooting, Old Lamont's repast was out of the question. Rome wanted them somewhere off the radar and safe.

"That was crazy," Nami finally said. "All those officers . . . the bodies on the ground. I—"

"Nope," Jelia cut off her daughter and shook her head. "I want the image of those lights flashing and all that blood out of my mind."

"But, Mama, it happened!"

"I know it did. But we're still here, and that's the only thing I want to discuss."

"Mama—"

"Nami, stop," Draya said and reached for Jelia's hand. "Today was already wild enough without replaying it out loud. That shit was terrifying."

"I know because *we* were the targets."

"No, your brother was the target," Jelia said.

"Same difference. If they would have killed us, it would be the same as killing him," Nami said and sighed. "It hasn't been like this in a minute. Old Lamont . . . Amari, DeJaun? You know I do both of their girlfriends' hair, right? It's just sad."

"Sad and dangerous. All we can do is pray for Rome and Dru's safety. They'll get things back right," Jelia said and sipped her wine.

"How . . . How do you do it?" Draya asked Jelia. "Knowing that at any moment, you might get a call saying one of them is gone?"

"The same way you do it, being with a man you know is in the streets. You trust 'em. You got to. My son is gonna take care of whoever was behind all of this. Believe that," Jelia said and tipped her glass at Draya.

Before Draya could say anything else, Pea came into the dining room and set their plates down in front of them. Pea was a pretty woman with a tongue sharp enough to slice a grapefruit. She had a no-nonsense attitude and knew how to run Rome's household like the back of her hand. And she was paid handsomely to do it. Although in her early forties, not a wrinkle could be seen on her smooth, caramel face, nor a gray hair on her head, most likely because she kept it dyed jet black. She was more fit than many women half her age, and her pear shape was still very much intact.

Born and raised in Chicago, Pea's grandmother had taught her how to cook and take care of a home at an early age while her granddaddy and brothers were out handling their business. Men made the money, women made the home. When she moved to Atlanta in her twenties, she had many skills to keep herself afloat. Housekeeping and nannying were just the ones that kept money rolling in. She was able to keep a roof over her head and stay in some of the finest places. Rome's home, she had to admit, was the most comfortable, mainly because the dynamic inside of it was something she was used to.

Pea was trying to be supportive of their experience. However, looking at their somber faces, she couldn't help but roll her eyes and sigh. After bringing them some lemonade to drink and placing the pitcher on the table, she put her hand on her hip.

"Next time, just wear a bulletproof vest," she said, shocking everyone.

"What did you just say?" Jelia asked, looking up at Pea, who rolled her eyes again.

"I said, next time, wear a bulletproof vest," she repeated herself. "Since you're so shaken up and scared, right? That would make more sense than you sitting at this table looking like scared children. Regardless of whether you like it, Rome ain't never hid what he does for a living from y'all or me. You all should have been more prepared, especially given the circumstances of what led to the funeral in the first place."

"Who are you talking to?" Draya asked, wrinkling her brow.

"The people your man left me to babysit," Pea said, and it was Draya's turn to roll her eyes.

"I—" Draya started, but stopped when her phone vibrated in her pocket. A tiny smile came over her face, and she pushed the cabbage away from her. "I'll eat later. This is my man. Jelia, Nami, you two have fun with her rude ass. You'll see what I'm talking about soon."

She got up from the table and left the kitchen to answer her phone. Pea turned back to Jelia and Nami, shaking her head at their pitiful expressions of sorrow.

"Death is a sad thing; survival is key. The funeral is over. You are still alive, but I don't know for how long if all you are gonna do is hide behind a car."

"What you sayin', Pea? That you woulda shot back?"

"Yes," Pea said matter-of-factly.

"Well, I'm not shooting no damn gun," Jelia said with a "*hmm.*"

"You *do* know Rome is a kingpin, *right?* People tend to shoot at those." Pea raised her brow at Jelia. "At some point, you *better* think about picking up a gun. I know Rome will protect you until he can't anymore, but you must know that, as his mother and sister, his enemies can reach him through you. Do you think he always has security around you for fun?"

"Well, who protects Draya? I've never seen one of his guys here," Nami said, waving her hands around.

"*Hm,*" Pea said with a smirk. "Come, let me show you something, little girl."

She wiped off her hands and removed her apron before exiting the kitchen. She didn't check to see if Nami was following her, but the sound of chair legs scraping back and forth let her know she was. Pea's quarters were on the first floor of the house toward the back. She was halfway there when she felt a small gust of air on her neck, and Nami caught up to her.

"Do you know why your brother hired me?"

"To clean and cook since Draya clearly doesn't do either," Nami answered, and Pea laughed.

"Draya is a sweet and beautiful girl, but she has no clue how to be a homemaker, so that *is* one reason I was hired. But do you know what got me the job over the other applicants?"

"Because you were the best for the job?"

"Yes, I was . . . but not just in the ways you think . . ."

Flashback . . .

1997

"Okay, ma'am, this is it," the young driver said, pulling into a desolate parking lot.

He looked into the rearview mirror at a suspicious-looking Pea in the backseat as she peered out of the window. Her brow furrowed, and she reached into her oversized purse to retrieve a small piece of paper with an address on it. She was dressed professionally and interview-ready. She had responded to an ad for a housekeeper in the paper and was happy when she got a call back after a week. The pay wasn't exactly what she was used to, but, being between jobs, she didn't want to let any opportunities slip by. She was also hoping for something that offered a room so she could get out of the rinky-dink apartment she was renting. However, had she known the interview would have been taking place somewhere like what she was looking at, she would have passed on it.

"This can't be right. This is an abandoned building," Pea said as she stared at a building that looked like it hadn't been used in ages. She looked back at the man driving the car. "You said your name is Melo, right? What the hell is this? I'm too damn old to get kidnapped."

She was extremely shocked. Especially given the fact that the employer had sent a car to pick her up. At first, she felt it was a good show of faith, but then she grew worried.

"Not everything is what it seems," Melo replied and unlocked the doors. "I'll be here to take you back home after your interview."

She stared back at him, contemplating what to do. She knew she was a good half hour from home, and even if she wanted to get out of the car and leave, she didn't have service on her phone to call anyone. If her granddaddy were still alive, he would be having a fit at how naïve she'd been to get into the stranger's car, no matter how nice it was. Not only that, but also all she had in her purse was some pepper spray and a switchblade.

"I . . . I don't know. Why would he have me meet him in a place like this?"

"Mr. Johnson don't like his address known to just anyone on the outside. It's safer for him this way. And what I need to say to you, Miss Pea, is he don't like to wait."

Pea hesitated for a few more seconds before she, against her better judgment, opened the door and stepped out into the blazing Georgia heat. She walked to the entrance and looked over her shoulder, surprised to see Melo still there. She was sure he would have driven off, but there he was, parked and reading the paper. That took a little tension off, but not much. Still, she remembered how strong a man her granddaddy had been and the way she'd watched him raise her and her brothers to be fearless. There were many worst-case scenarios, but on the other hand, Melo might have been telling the truth. And if he was, that meant the employer had a nice chunk of change. The truth was, even though odds were against it, she didn't want to risk missing out on a good job opportunity.

She pulled on the heavy door, but her other foot caught it before it shut completely when she was inside. Pea looked around the well-lit interior and saw what appeared to be an unused clothing warehouse, echoing with silence. The air was heavy with the scent of aged textiles, mingled with a subtle must of indicative neglect. Light peeked in through the high windows from the sun outside, casting shadows across the remnants of fabric, detached labels and hangers. She observed the empty rows of shelving units on the walls and the debris-strewn floor. She almost turned around, thinking it was the perfect setting for a horror film, but the sound of someone laughing stopped her. It wasn't a sinister laugh. It was a humorous one, and it was coming from straight ahead.

Pea turned her focus to the back of the warehouse, where she saw a handsome, young man come from around a corner. He didn't look older than his early twenties, but he wore designer clothes from head to toe. On his neck was a thick, gold chain, and hanging from it was a diamond-encrusted "C" pendant.

"I don't have any money, if y'all lured me here to rob me," Pea told him. "And if you try, I'll slice you ear to ear."

"It look like I need to rob you?" he asked, flexing the watch on his wrist before laughing again.

"Then what do you want from me?"

"Didn't you respond to my ad in the paper?"

"Yeah. But it said you were looking for a housekeeper. This ain't no damn house."

"Trust me, there's a house. But to get there, you gotta go through the process. So, do you want to continue the interview or not, Peoria Lily Myrtle?"

Her eyes widened slightly at the mention of her full legal name. She had never made mention of that. She said that her name was Pea Little when she responded to the ad. Seeing her shock, the young man chuckled again.

"The only Pea Little in Atlanta died in 1985. And she was a white woman, so I know you couldn't have stolen her identity. So, that meant that wasn't your real name. I did some diggin', and what I came up with impressed me."

"Why? I can't imagine someone so young could know who I am."

"You? Nah, I don't know much about you . . . yet. But tell me who was Otis Myrtle to you?"

"He was my grandfather."

"And Brutus and Jameer Myrtle?"

"My brothers."

"Damn. The stories my uncle used to tell me about them when I was a kid. He said Otis Little was the biggest boss to come from New Orleans. Those stories spread for miles and miles. He said one time, he hung some people by their toes who owed him money. Is that true?"

Pea nodded, remembering that night like it was yesterday. She and her grandmother had just finished setting the table when her granddaddy and brothers walked through the door with blood splatters on their clothes. As soon as she saw them, she knew the drill. Burn the clothes and never talk about what happened.

"They weren't stories to me . . . That was my real life," Pea said, finally letting the door shut all the way. "It's not a normal life. It was a hard one."

"Hard or not, I bet y'all had everything you could ever dream of."

"We did. 'Til that same life caught up to my granddaddy and my brothers," Pea said sadly, thinking about the moment she found out they were dead. "When they were killed, my grandma's heart couldn't take it. Nothing was the same anymore because, how could it be? I tried to fill the emptiness in her heart, but I couldn't. She knew she could lose my granddaddy any day to that life, but maybe deep down, she just didn't believe he could die. I don't think any of us did. And then to lose her only grandsons the same night? It was bad. She felt like she didn't have a purpose no more, even though I was still living. She died shortly after them, broken heart. She left everything to me, but I didn't want it. I sold it and left it all behind me. Moved to Atlanta and adapted to the accent out here so no one would link me back to that life."

"Well, those stories—"

"Nightmares," Pea corrected.

"Depends on who's talkin' bout 'em. Needless to say, those stories inspired my uncle's operation, and his operation inspired mine," the young man said, and Pea scoffed.

"It makes sense then. The driver, the warehouse, the jewelry. You're a drug dealer, just like my granddaddy was, huh? What's your name?"

"Rome," he said with confidence, and she was even more shocked.

The name rang quite a bell because she'd heard it so much over the years. If he was the Rome she was thinking of, then he was the one who ran a big part of Atlanta. He had a lot of love and respect in the streets, the kind that had made her think he was much older than the person in front of her.

"How old are you, Rome? You can't be more than 20."

"I'm around there. But age don't mean shit in this life, but as young as your brothers were, I'm sure you know that. The difference is I'm the boss. Ain't nobody over me. And I'm lookin' to hire someone for this position who I ain't gotta hide who I am from."

"You got children?"

"Nah, not yet. But I got a girl who could use some help in the house I just bought."

"Hmm . . . That's all you need me to do?"

Rome looked at her, and a small smile formed on his face at what was implied in her question. As she looked at him, there was something that seemed familiar. She didn't know if it was how he seemed so sure of himself or the way his eyes never left her as he spoke. But for a second, she felt her grandfather's energy in the room. A short silence echoed before he motioned with his head for her to follow him. That time, Pea didn't hesitate at all. He waited for her to make her way across to the warehouse before leading her down the hallway from which he had come. They walked side by side, passing a few doors on both sides.

"Where are we going?" Pea asked curiously, as the hallway seemed to go on forever.

"You'll see. But first, I want to tell you about the job. It pays twenty thousand monthly. Room and board included."

"Twenty thousand?" *Her eyes widened at hearing such a hefty amount.*

"Yeah, 'cause I don't need no ordinary housekeeper. I need someone who won't just keep the crib clean. I need to know that you'll protect it and any person in it."

"You don't have security for that? Male security?"

"I do, but the home is the holder of secrets. It's some shit not just anybody should have access to. I don't like people in my house like that. The same person I trust to shoot for me in the streets might not be one I want around my lady or near my safe."

"How do you know you can trust me?" Pea asked when they stopped in front of a door at the end of the long hallway.

"I don't . . . yet," Rome said and paused. He looked Pea so deeply into her eyes that she almost had to catch her breath. "There was another story my uncle told me: home evasion, 1969. Three robbers entered the home of an elderly woman while her husband was gone. They viciously beat her, demandin' to know where her husband kept his money. In the midst of that shit, a teenage girl came home from school and saw her grandmother bloody on the kitchen floor. She told the robbers she would take them to the safe, and she did. Only, there wasn't money inside it. There was only a chrome revolver that she pulled out and shot all three of them dead in her grandfather's office."

His words hung in the air, visible almost, like a heat haze above asphalt, as Pea remembered taking the lives of those three thieves. At the time, she thought she'd never forget their faces for as long as she lived, but there she was, having difficulty remembering even the color of their eyes. Afterward, her granddaddy had told her how proud he was of her, and the first time he killed somebody, he realized that it just went to the back of his mind because he would always do what he needed to do to ensure his future and that of the ones he loved.

"Just don't think about it. And when you finally do think about it, you'll have forgotten," he'd said to her. "Remember that, because this might not be the last time you have to use a gun."

And it wasn't. In fact, there were many more times, like when her brother Brutus picked her up from school and took her along to make a pickup. He made a rookie mistake by leaving his gun in the glove box and almost got robbed by someone he trusted. If it weren't for Pea grabbing the gun and shooting from the car, Brutus would have had a knife in his back as he was walking away. There was also another time with her brother Jameer that was so bloody she never tried to recall it. Sometimes she wondered if she'd been there the night they were killed, would it have made a difference? When she moved, she put that life behind her, but there it was, knocking at her door, and she'd gone right to it.

"H . . . How do you know the revolver was chrome? That wasn't a detail I told the police when they came."

"I didn't. Me and my unc just envisioned it like that," Rome grinned, but then his face grew serious. "I'm sorry you lost ya whole family. I don't ever wanna know what that feels like. But if you want the job, I'll give you a new family, protection and put some bread in your pocket. All I ask for in return is your loyalty. What do you say?"

"I accept," Pea found herself saying without even thinking.

"Good. So tell me, is that shit still in you, or did the old Peoria Lily Myrtle die back then too?"

"She's . . . I'm still me."

"Prove it," he said and opened the door in front of them.

When Pea looked inside, she was taken aback to see a man bound and gagged in an empty room. He'd been beaten badly. The floor surrounding him was bloody. He looked like he was barely clinging to life. When he saw her standing there, hope flashed in his eyes, and he began trying to say something, but it just came out as moans.

"What did he do?"

"He tried to kill me," Rome said and removed a gun from his hip. "So, what do you think I should d—"

Before he could finish his sentence, Pea snatched the gun from his hands and shot the man in the head right between the eyes. His pleading sounds were turning her stomach. She just wanted to put him out of his misery. She handed the gun back to a smirking Rome and let out a breath.

"So, do I have the job?"

Present Day . . .

By the time Pea finished the story, Nami was wearing a look of wonder on her face. They had long since reached Pea's room and were sitting on her bed as she recounted the day she first met Rome. Nami had been silent the whole time, but at the end, she gasped.

"You *killed* him?"

"That's what I said, didn't I?" Pea asked, getting up from the bed and going to her bedroom dresser. "I knew that once I let that warehouse door shut, I was already too deep down the rabbit hole to go back, and I was all right with that. When you choose to go forward, you go forward."

"What does that even mean?"

"It means if you accept the life your brother comes with, along with all the shiny things, you are a part of it." Pea opened the top drawer, pulled out a .22, then took it to Nami and handed it to her. "Then you better be ready to fight alongside him to keep it. Especially now that Slaw started a fucking war."

Chapter 12

"Uh-uh. I changed my mind. I don't want my ends bumped. Can you make them straight again?"

It took everything in Nami not to weaponize the flat iron in her hand and burn her client with it. It was the third request the woman had made, and every time, Nami did as she was asked. And yet, the client didn't like it. All of Nami's classmates were packing up their work equipment for the day and preparing to head home. On Fridays, Nami and her classmates took clients at their school, but they didn't charge for their services. Although the clients could tip, the service was on the house, and the workday went toward her credit hours. Nami held in her sigh and forced a smile on her face, reminding herself that she needed all her hours and no complaints.

"Of course, Miss Victoria, but after this, I have to go," Nami said sweetly to the middle-aged Black woman.

She was a pretty, full-figured woman who never missed a Friday to come and get her hair done for free. Nami should have been used to how picky she was, but that day, she was being *extremely* particular. What was supposed to have been a simple trim and flat iron had turned into much more. It honestly wouldn't have taken as long, but Victoria found out that Nami was a good braider too. She asked her to put cornrows on the left side of her head, then flat-iron the right. Of course, Nami obliged, but she was ready to go.

"Oops, my bad. Am I interrupting your weekend plans?" Victoria asked and then raised one of her brows nosily. "Maybe with a special sexy somebody?"

"What?" Nami found herself laughing as she ran the flat iron over her hair. "Miss Victoria, I'm single. I don't have a sexy nothin' nowhere."

"And you're young too, but still, if I still had a body like yours, ain't no way I wouldn't be on the arm of one or two fine young men. *Mmm.* I used to have quite the time in my day."

"Miss Victoria, you say that like you're old. You still look good." Nami finished up and handed her a mirror.

"Baby, I never said all that." Miss Victoria admired her reflection, finally seeming satisfied with her head. "I'm just talking about my single days. I was a trip and a half. Had these motherfuckas chasing this pussy up a tree, okay?"

"Well, what happened?"

"Chile, I got married." Miss Victoria rolled her eyes and pursed her lips.

"You are a mess," Nami said, laughing again, taking the mirror from her.

She removed the cape from over Miss Victoria and let her stand. Nami admired her handiwork from the front, and she had to admit she'd done a good job. She couldn't wait to have her degree so she could open her own hair shop.

"And you? You're a liar," Miss Victoria said after handing Nami a twenty-dollar tip.

"What you mean, I'm a liar?"

"You said you didn't have anybody. If not, who's that sexy motherfucka right there looking at you like he wanna eat ya?" she asked and pointed.

"What?" Nami asked, then followed her finger to the door of the school salon.

Leaning against it and indeed staring at her intently was Jyair. As usual, he was fine as wine and well dressed. His hair was in two neat cornrows, and he had a fresh shape-up. His shirt was slightly unbuttoned, showcasing the tattoos on his chest and arms. While she genuinely was shocked to see him, she wasn't surprised to see one of her brother's guys there to pick her up. Lately, Rome hadn't wanted her to go anywhere by herself, especially since her Jeep was so well-known in the city. He'd been having Triston look after her since the drive-by. In fact, he was the one who had dropped her off at school that morning, so she hadn't expected to see Jyair standing there, waiting for her.

"*Mm-hmm,*" Miss Victoria said when she saw the smile on Nami's face.

"I'll see you next time, Miss Victoria," Nami said, trying to hide her giggle. She put Miss Victoria's money into her Chanel bag. "Make sure you wrap your hair so you don't have to keep puttin' heat on it."

Miss Victoria walked to the exit, her eyes never leaving Jyair. Nami couldn't blame her. He was a nice sight to see. When she was gone, Nami straightened up and packed her workstation. She heard footsteps behind her and, looking over her shoulder, saw Jyair approaching. He took her equipment bag from her so he could carry it, and she grabbed her purse.

"Thank you," she said as they walked out of the school salon. He held the door for her and let her go through first. "Why you here anyway? I thought Triston was comin' back to get me."

"Ro want me with you from now on," Jyair said, surprising her.

"Really? Who's with Mama then?"

"Melo. Ro figured he should be the one on full-time duty with her since he can't be active in the streets for real until he heals up."

"How he gon' protect my mama with a fucked-up arm?"

"He only need one to shoot," Jyair said.

"Hmm . . . interesting," she said, and the doubt must have been apparent in her voice.

"What, you don't think I'm good enough to keep you safe?" he asked, making an offended expression.

"No, I—"

"So, I'm good enough to protect yo' mama, but not you is what you sayin'?"

"Jyair, that's *not* what I was sayin' at all. I—" She stopped midsentence when she saw and heard him crack up, laughing. "You play too damn much."

"My bad, I just had to mess with you one time. Here, let me get ya door," he said and went to the passenger side of his Mustang.

When he did so, she got a whiff of his cologne. He smelled just as good as he looked. Nami tried to tame the butterflies in her stomach before he got into the car. She couldn't remember the last time she had a crush like that. When he climbed in, he started the car and drove toward her apartment. Realizing that, Nami made a face.

"How you know where I live?" she asked, and he looked at her like she was off her rocker.

"You *do* know who yo' brother is, right? Even before all this, he made sure you was good at all times. Especially at the crib."

She felt a rush of affection toward her brother. He really would do anything to keep them all safe. However, she realized the privacy she thought she had was just an illusion. She looked out the window, wondering if Jyair had been on duty the night she'd gotten picked up for dates.

"You shouldn't just be lettin' motherfuckas know where you lay your head at, by the way," he said as if he were reading her thoughts.

"What you mean?"

"Dude in the gray old school. He took you to that Italian restaurant you and your mom like."

"You followed us to the restaurant?"

"Why would I stay posted outside of the crib if the purpose of me watchin' the crib is 'cause you're in it?" he asked.

"Don't be makin' up no excuses for stalkin' me," Nami teased, and Jyair shook his head as he drove. She could see he was fighting the smile coming to his lips.

"For real, though, don't be havin' no dudes pick you up from yo' spot. You don't know what they're after. Everybody knows whose sister you are. Plus, if one of these weirdos did somethin' to you, I'd . . ." He let his voice trail.

"You'd what?"

"Nothin', you hungry?"

"I could eat."

Jyair switched lanes and turned down a street that led to a Jamaican restaurant popular for its jerk chicken and oxtails. Since it was Friday, a good-sized crowd was there. When he parked, he got out and opened her door for her. Nami was glad she decided to be cute for class that day. Her low-rise jeans and pink handkerchief tie top showed off her perfectly sculpted body. She looked good walking next to him into the restaurant, and she knew it. She liked that he didn't let her touch a door and how he naturally took her hand to lead her to a cozy booth upholstered in a colorful fabric. They sat across from each other and started looking at the menu. It didn't take long for their server to come and take their drink orders.

"I think I'm just gonna do the jerk chicken, rice and cabbage," Nami said.

"Me too," Jyair said, closing his menu and putting it aside.

Nami turned her head to look around the restaurant. It was like stepping into a vibrant slice of the Caribbean. The walls were painted in the bright, warm colors of yellow, green and red and covered in murals depicting Jamaican life. She noticed the swaying palm trees and legendary reggae icons. Of course, Bob Marley was in the center. She danced slightly to the reggaeton playing softly, and by the time her eyes made it back to Jyair, she almost looked away again.

"What?" she asked, seeing his eyes were intensely on her.

"Nothin', you just look good under this light," he told her, and she rolled her eyes.

"Jyair, you probably say that to every girl you date," she said back.

"Oh, so this a date?"

"I didn't say all that now. I barely know anything about you, for real. I mean, I know you work for my brother, you get money and you seem sweet. But I done heard a lot of other stories too."

"Like what?"

"That you a killer," she said, thinking he was going to shy away from the subject, but instead, he merely shrugged.

"This shit is eat or be eaten. I'll do whatever I gotta do to make it home."

"Is that why Ro got you protectin' me?"

"He either felt I was the best man for the job, or . . ." He looked her in her eyes.

"Or what?"

"He knows that I like you . . . a lot. And knows I'ma protect you with everything in me." His eyes averted to something over her shoulder. "Like right now—*duck!*"

Nami didn't think twice. She ducked down just as she heard the sound of a gun going off and felt the air of a bullet whizzing past her head. Jyair's gun was already drawn, and he returned fire. Nami could hear the screams of the people around her in the restaurant over the gunfire, but she didn't dare lift her head. Suddenly, the gunfire stopped, and she felt a strong hand grab her arm and tug her.

"Come on. They ran out," Jyair said in a hurried tone.

Nami lifted her head and looked around at the damage done to the restaurant. There were bullet holes in the walls, and some of the glass windows were shattered. The other customers were on the ground covering their heads with their hands. She got up and ran out of the restaurant with Jyair, whose gun was still drawn, looking around to make sure no one was following them. When they got back to his car, he opened the door to let her in.

However, as he was doing so, a white car sped through the parking lot toward them. The hair on the back of Nami's neck stood up when she saw the glint of the pistol in the driver's hand, and instinct took over. She reached into her purse and pulled out the handgun given to her by Pea and aimed it at the car as it passed. Before the driver could shoot, she fired at the car, forcing them to swerve violently and speed away. She felt Jyair snatch her up, put her in the car, then get in himself and drive away from the restaurant.

Nami was still in shock and looking down at the gun in her hand as he drove. When they were a good distance away, he pulled over and came to an abrupt stop. Turning to face her, he cupped her cheek with one hand and made her look at him. When she did, he studied her.

"You okay?" he asked, and she nodded.

"I . . . I don't know. Who was that?" she asked breathlessly.

"Twan. One of Slaw's boys." He looked down at the gun in her hand. "Where you get this from?"

"It doesn't matter."

"Yeah, well, it's my job to protect you. Not the other way around. Next time, get the fuck out of the way. You coulda got shot, Nami."

"He coulda killed you. I . . . I . . ." Nami's voice trembled.

"I don't need you tryin'a be a hero, understand?" Jyair asked, and when she didn't say anything, he got louder. "Do you *hear* me?"

She didn't like him yelling at her, but she heard the fear in his voice and saw the worry in his eyes as they scanned her face, stopping on her lips. She felt him pull her face close to his at the exact moment she naturally leaned into him. Their lips met, and they shared a kiss of both desire and longing. Nami wished it could last forever because, for a moment, she forgot about the world around her.

"Don't do that again, okay?" he whispered when they parted, and he stroked her cheek tenderly.

She nodded, although she knew she was lying. She wished she could tell him that she wouldn't, but her actions had been automatic. It was then that she realized she would do anything to protect the people she cared about. Even kill. Pea had been right. There were some things she wouldn't be able to get around, especially being Rome's sister. She couldn't even enjoy a simple lunch without someone wanting to kill her. There was no way she'd completely put her life in someone else's hands if her own hands worked. She didn't say anything. Instead, she just tucked the gun away in her purse and leaned back in her seat as he started driving again.

Chapter 13

"I thought we were going out tonight?" Draya's voice snuck up on Rome as he was tucking in his chain.

He looked over his shoulder from where he stood in their shared quarters and saw her standing there in a short jean skirt that clung to her wide hips and a black cowl neck crop top. She wore heels and had her purse on her shoulder, looking ready to go. The loud look of disappointment on her face overshadowed her beauty as she stared at his clothing. The all-black sweat suit with matching black Air Force 1s was very telling. He had no plans to go on a date that night.

"My bad, baby, we can go out tomorrow night," he told her, and she rolled her eyes.

"No, we can't go out tomorrow. You *do* know tonight's the last night of the comedy show, and you promised weeks ago you'd take me."

In truth, he did remember promising to take her to the show, but that was before Old Lamont got killed, and so much began happening in the streets. It had been a little over a week since Old Lamont's funeral, and although things seemed to have settled down, that was what Rome wanted everyone to think. Unlike Slaw's back-to-back mayhem, Rome didn't like making moves in the heat. He wanted to be calculated and strike right when everyone had just begun to relax.

"Take one of your girls in my place, baby. I'ma be out late tonight."

"You know I'm really getting sick and tired of coming in second to the streets, Ro."

"You knew what you was signin' up for when you decided to be with me," he said a little more harsh than intended.

"And back then, you seemed to have more time for me," Draya spat back. "What, was that just some little game to reel me in? You probably got some other bitch out there that you're dropping dick off to 'cause you sure ain't gave me none."

"I ain't got no other bitch. You my only one." Rome whipped around to face her just in time to see her eyebrows rise to the ceiling.

"Oh, so I'm a bitch now?"

"You know what I meant," he sighed and walked up to her, but she swatted away his outstretched arms. "And see, that's the reason you ain't got no dick. Every time I try, you push me away."

"Because that be the only time you want to spend time with me," Draya said, her bottom lip trembling slightly. "Yeah, you give me money to do whatever, but lately, I do everything alone. I'm tired of it."

"After I dead this shit with Slaw, shit will go back to normal, baby. I need you to trust me on that. But more importantly, I need you to *be* here. Support yo' man. If I don't handle what I need to handle out there in them streets, we won't even have a home. And after that, I got a move that's gon' get us outta the game for good."

"For good?" Draya's face lit up. "Like, completely legit?"

"Forever legit," he said earnestly, and she smiled.

That time, when he tried to pull her in close, she let him. He didn't hesitate to kiss her the second she looked into his face. The feel of her full, soft lips on his instantly activated an appetite inside of him that hadn't been satisfied in a while. She smiled into his mouth when she felt his erection grow against her. Pulling away slightly, she batted her lashes sexily at him, letting him know she wanted him too.

"How much time you got before the show starts?" he asked in a low tone.

"Enough . . ."

He pulled her back into another kiss. That one deeper, hungrier and more passionate as their tongues danced around each other. Her hands found their way up his chest and around the back of his neck, while he hiked up her skirt and squeezed her round bottom. He wanted to completely undress her and make love to every part of her body, but time on both ends wouldn't allow it.

Without warning, Draya lowered herself down on her heels and pulled down Rome's pants and boxers. His one-eyed monster was standing at attention and didn't stand a chance against getting devoured by her deep throat. Her mouth was so wet and warm that Rome felt chills up his back as she tried to swallow his tip whole. Her head game was one of the reasons Rome knew he had to have her. She was so nasty and sloppy with it that sometimes he couldn't even make it into her cat before he exploded. He gripped her head as it bobbed back and forth and proceeded to thrust powerfully, fucking her face. She barely gagged on his thick eight inches, but by then, she was used to his size and a pro at pleasing him.

"Shit, Draya," he hissed through his teeth.

The sounds of her sucking and slurping, along with the feeling of it, had him on cloud nine. He knew that he was close to exploding in her mouth, and although it was one of the best feelings ever, he wanted to please her too. Gently cupping her chin with his hands, he forced her back to her feet.

"Your turn," he said and spun her around.

Bending her over one of the dressers in their bedroom, he hiked up her skirt some more and moved her thong to the side. Draya's cat was so fat that her plump lips closed completely even if her legs were open. He could see her juices glistening and dripping from the slit, and he felt himself throbbing from wanting to be inside her. But before that could happen, he just had to have a taste. Dropping down, Rome took a handful of her cheeks in both hands and spread them before diving in face-first.

"Baby," Draya cried, feeling his tongue slip and slide through her pussy and up to her crack.

She felt herself bend over more as her body relaxed into him. She shivered when he began circling the thumb of one hand over her clit and thrusted in and out of her with the middle finger from his other hand as his tongue flicked over her butthole. Her orgasm was ineluctable. She gave a loud, sexy moan as she gushed all over Rome's hand, but he wouldn't let her tap out then. Before she was even completely done releasing, he stood up and shoved all eight inches into her drenched tunnel. He felt her tight walls try to resist his entrance, begging for him to give her body time to recover, but it was too late. He was already inside.

He pounded into her relentlessly, and her hands flailed around on the dresser, trying to grip something—anything. He lost track of how many times she whimpered his name. He was too busy watching her bottom shake when he crashed into it. He only averted his gaze when Draya looked back at him with a pleasured grimace on her face and lowered eyes.

"I love you, Rome," she said through pouted lips, and that was what did it.

"Fuck," he shouted as his body jerked.

He was deep inside of her when his soldiers shot from his tip, and he didn't bother trying to pull out. He held her tightly until the electrifying sensation passed, and he felt all his energy fade. Once he was emptied, he finally removed himself and stumbled back onto the bed. He fell on his back and closed his eyes, trying to catch his breath. A few moments later, he felt a warm towel on him, and when he opened his eyes, he saw Draya wiping her juices off him.

"Can't have you out there handling business sticky and smelling like pussy," she said with a grin.

"Thank you," he said, returning her grin.

When she finished, he pulled up his pants. She then went to the dresser, grabbed her purse and a new pair of panties and went into the bathroom. He heard some water running and knew she was freshening up for the night. He heard her on the phone with someone, but couldn't make out what she was saying. However, by the time she came out, a look of excitement was on her face.

"What?"

"Tika said she would go with me, so I guess I won't have to curse you out."

"That dick I just dropped made sure you wasn't gon' curse me out," he said, laughing. "I'ma have one of the guys tail y'all there."

"No, I don't want a security guard, plus that shit scares my friends. Makes them not want to hang out with me because they think I got a target on my back." Her eyes plead with Rome.

"I don't like the thought of you bein' out here naked like that, shawty."

"I'll be fine. I promise I'll come right home after. Just let me be normal for one night, and tomorrow you can have your boys protect me like I'm the first lady of the United States."

He didn't like it, and everything in him was screaming no. But he knew the pressure he had been putting on her, and he wasn't a fool. He knew she was unhappy, and he not going to the show just added to that. Before giving her an answer, he got off the bed and went to the closet. When he came out, he held a small handgun.

"If you want to go without one of my guys there, you gotta carry this. You remember how I taught you to shoot it?"

"Yes," she beamed and took the gun. "But I won't need to use it. I'ma be all right, trust me."

She stepped on her tiptoes and gave him a few pecks on the lips. When she pulled away, she put her nose to his upper lip and inhaled. A giggle escaped her mouth before kissing him one last time.

"Make sure you wash your face too before you leave," she said with a wink and made her way to the door.

"Draya?" Rome said before she left. She looked over her shoulder. "I love you too."

She blew him a kiss before walking out of the room. When she was gone, Rome went to the bathroom and washed her sweet smell from his mouth. After he brushed his teeth, he exited the bathroom, and his eyes instantly flew to the digital clock in the room. It read seven thirty, and he knew he had to get a move on it. He left the room and was halfway down the stairs when he felt his phone vibrating in his pocket. Pulling it out, he wasn't surprised to see Dru's contact on the screen.

"I'm leavin' the crib now," he said as soon as he answered.

"Good. Me and Jyair about to pull up to the warehouse now."

"Where's Melo?"

"Already at the spot, keepin' a eye out."

"Cool. I'ma be up with y'all in a second."

Rome disconnected the call and continued downstairs and out of the house. With each step he took, he felt himself growing colder and colder inside. Ever since he had come into the game, he'd been fighting, and now that he had finally gotten to the top, he was fighting to stay there. He thought he had finally reached a moment of peace, and everybody was eating. But Slaw had flexed his power, or the power he thought he had, and Rome knew it was time to show him exactly who was running the show.

Chapter 14

"Baby, fuck . . . That shit feels *so* good."

The blissful screams belonged to Camilla James, Milla for short. She was a beautiful woman with a curly, pixie cut and coconut-colored complexion. Sweat drenched her back as she straddled and rode the love of her life as if she were in the wild, wild west. It always felt like heaven when he was inside of her, and as always, she aimed to please him. His hands roughly explored her body as she tried to get him to release his whole day inside of her.

Finally, he tossed her off of him and pinned her down on her back, placing his hands behind her knees, forcing them to her shoulders. With her legs wide open and her completely helpless, he slid back into her and pounded away until she squirted liquid everywhere. She tried to speak and tell him how much she loved him, but nothing but jumbled words came out. She stared up into his focused face, and her feelings for him were evident on her face. He brought her to two more orgasms before he finally released his own. Hurrying to pull out, he jacked the tip of his manhood off until he came messily all over her stomach. Milla smacked her lips and rolled her eyes.

"You know you coulda let that go inside of me," she said seductively and grabbed a towel from her silver nightstand to wipe the cum away.

"I'm not stupid. I know you been plotting on having another baby," he said and lay next to her on the bed.

"Our son is so cute. We should try to see what our faces look like on a girl," Milla said, snuggling up to him, ignoring the fact that he didn't even attempt to pull her closer.

In fact, the closeness she'd felt just moments before faded the second he released his load. He stared at the ceiling, lost in thought, not paying her words any mind. She sighed and gently stroked the side of his handsome face. Milla hated how, even when near, he felt like he was at a distance, because the truth was, she didn't want anyone else. His silence was killing her. It was like he was in the room alone. Like he hadn't just screwed her brains out.

"Slaw, do you love me?" she heard herself ask.

He was the father of her son, and for her, the love of her life. When she met him three years ago, she was running drugs for him. Being kicked out at 18 by a jealous mother and having to turn to the streets, Milla needed a quick way to make money. And that was the only way she knew how. When they started sleeping together, it wasn't anything serious. It was just sex. But when Milla ended up pregnant, Slaw took her off the streets and put her in her own apartment. He made sure she didn't want for anything, and when their son was born two years ago, she thought they would be a family, especially since he was over at her place several times a week with them. But although her lifestyle had changed, and she was living well, there was one thing that seemed to remain the same. Nothing between her and Slaw seemed to grow. Nothing seemed serious. It felt like she was stuck in that same beginning loop with him as before they had their son.

"Why?" Slaw finally asked.

"Because it's been three years, and you still seem so cold to me. I want us to be a family," she said hopefully. "You know Cairo loves you."

"Of course, he loves me. I'm his dad," Slaw said flatly, addressing only the part that he wanted to. "I love him too."

"What about me?" She looked at him in time to see him close his eyes and inhale deeply.

"I got you the crib, the car, a purse full of money and everything in your closet. You don't gotta work. What more do you want from me?"

"I want *you*. Don't you understand that?" Her voice wavered, seeing how uninterested he was in the conversation.

"I don't know how many times you want me to spare your feelings, Milla. But this was never that."

"Never what? *Huh?* If you don't love me, then why do you do all this shit for me?" Her voice grew louder with each word.

"A fairy tale. Except me and you were never going to ride off into the sunset. I do what I do for you for one reason only: Cairo."

"C-Cairo?" she asked.

"Yeah, my son. I didn't do any of this until you told me you were pregnant. I wanted the best for him. I didn't pull you off the streets for you; I did it for him. I buy you nice clothes so you can look good enough to represent him. The car, the crib and the money is all for him. The pussy you give me is just a bonus, but I could do without that."

His words stung her so deeply that she couldn't even respond. She pulled away from him and just stared with watery eyes. Milla was still trying to figure out what to say when he got a phone call that he took right there in her bed.

"What's up, you good?" he answered, perking up a bit. He paused and listened to what the person on the other end of the phone was saying. "Okay. Yeah, I'll be there. Let me throw some clothes on."

He hung up, and Milla was in utter disbelief. She felt the anger growing inside her as she watched him get out of bed and go into her closet, where he kept some things. She jumped out of bed and hurried after him.

"Motherfucka, did you just answer the phone for a bitch in *my* bed?" she shouted at his back as he grabbed a pair of slacks and a shirt.

"I did," he answered dryly.

"We *just* got done fucking!"

"So?"

"And you about to go see a bitch? Right now?"

"I'ma shower first."

The breath Milla took felt like it sliced her tongue all the way to the back of her throat. She saw red and didn't even think of stopping her fists from flying at him. She was much smaller than he was, standing at a mere five foot four, and her fists were tiny, but she swung with all her might. She heard the thuds of her hand hitting his back, and when he turned swiftly to face her, she aimed at his face. He caught her fist midair and restrained her other wrist as well.

"Do you feel better?" he asked, unfazed by her loss of control.

"I hate you!" she spat, and he smirked.

"You don't. You wish you did, though."

It was the truth. Even at that moment, she longed for him to take his words back and just get into bed with her. Tears welled up in her eyes as she stared into his cold eyes. She didn't understand why he didn't want her the way she wanted him. She tried to hit him again, but his grip on her was too strong.

"Get your shit and get the fuck out of my crib," she said through gritted teeth. "You don't ever have to come back.

If you're gonna have bitches, I'll get me a new man. Give my son a new dad."

Those were the only words she said that evoked any kind of emotion in him, and it wasn't the one she wanted. Fury flashed over his face, and before she knew it, he had a hand around her throat, squeezing the life out of her. He pushed her into one of the walls of the closet and pressed his forehead into hers.

"I don't give a fuck what you do with that pussy. But if you ever have another man around my son, I'll kill you. Do you understand?" he growled like a bear. He jerked her hard, causing her to whimper. "Do you?"

"Y-yeah," she choked out with her eyes clenched shut.

Red-hot tears fell down her cheeks as she gasped for air. He hadn't loosened his grip yet, and she was scared to open her eyes to look at him. It was the first time he'd ever put his hands on her, although she knew very well what he was capable of. From the murderous horror stories whispered around his name wherever he went, she knew he was dangerous, but right then, she *felt* it. There was a demon that lived inside that man, and at that moment, she knew it had completely consumed him. She said a silent prayer to herself that he didn't kill her right then and there. Finally, she felt him come close to her and place his lips by her ear.

"Until my son becomes a man, I *own* you," he hissed and then finally let her go.

Milla dropped to her knees, sobbing and choking on her spit. Her lungs were so grateful for the air she was sending to them. Her hands flew to her sore neck. She had never felt so weak in her life. Slaw barely gave her a second look as he stepped around her and exited the closet.

Chapter 15

The night was growing old, but the parking lot of the Kent's Corner Store was packed. Loud music was playing, people were outside their cars talking and laughing, girls were dancing and the air smelled like the best weed in the city. That kind of crowd wasn't abnormal, since there were many popular bars in the area, and Kent's was where people often hung out before and after. Scoping out the scene to make sure no one was there who wasn't supposed to be, and serving their regular customers were Mac and Twan. The two of them leaned against the building, passing a blunt back and forth. After taking a long draw, Twan burst out laughing out of nowhere.

"Man, what the fuck yo' high ass laughin' about?" Mac asked, looking at him like something was wrong with him.

"I was just thinkin' bout how fast Rome hit the concrete outside the church," Twan said and laughed some more.

At first, Mac was mad about the failed drive-by attempt, but thinking back to how fast they made Rome drop made him laugh too. It was proof that they'd truly caught him slipping, and if they could do it once, then they could do it again. They would just have to wait for the opportunity to present itself.

"If it wasn't for Dru's bitch ass, I woulda kept shootin'," Mac said, shaking his head.

"Aye, you think we goin' to hell for shootin' outside of a church?" Twan asked with a serious look on his face.

"Man, give me this shit, high ass," Mac laughed again and snatched the blunt from Twan's fingers. "It's a lot of other reasons why I know I'm goin' to hell, but at least I know all the homies gon' be there."

"Fa sho," Twan said, and the two of them slapped hands. "I told you I almost got Jyair the other day?"

"Almost?" Mac asked, and Twan smacked his lips.

"Yeah. I forgot that motherfucka got aim, though. I had to get scarce and fast." Suddenly, Twan saw something in the distance and made a face. "Damnnn, look at shawty right there."

Mac turned around and knew immediately who he was talking about. A sexy redbone with long legs and tall stilettos was walking through the crowded parking lot, headed right for them. She was wearing a short skirt over her plump bottom, making every man's head turn as she passed. Covering her perky breasts was a halter top that had a cherry on it. She wore her hair in long blond braids and had the face of an angel. Mac was so transfixed with her, he didn't even notice LuLu walking right alongside her.

"You Mac?" she asked when they were directly in front of him.

Her hazel brown eyes never left his and seemed to speak a language of their own. Mac took another drag from the blunt and put it out on the building behind him. Before answering her, he blew the smoke out slightly to the side so it just lightly brushed her cheek.

"Yeah, I'm Mac. Whose askin'?"

"Me clearly," she said with a slight smirk.

"And who's 'me'?"

"My name is Erica."

"Erica, I like that," Mac said and looked at LuLu's tattered appearance. "What you doin' rollin' with a dope fiend?"

"This dope fiend is my auntie," Erica said, rolling her neck. "And she wanna know why you won't sell to her no more. I know the money good. I'm the one who gave it to her."

"You the one who been givin' her the money to buy her dope?" Mac wrinkled his brows, and Erica held up her hand.

"Yeah, and before you judge me, this is my favorite auntie, and she looked out for me. Now, I wanna see her in a rehab, but I'd rather see her happy."

"You need somethin' too?"

"Nah, I don't fuck with the rock. I fuck with the powder, though," Erica said and licked her pearly whites in Mac's face. "So, what you gon' do? You gon' be her supplier again, 'cause I can't keep getting up and coming all the way over here for this shit?"

"Yeah, Mac, what you gon' do?" LuLu asked, quickly looking around as if something might get her at any moment.

"What *you* willin' to do to make sure I supply this dope fiend?" Mac asked Erica. "They don't call me Big Dick Mac for nothin'. My truck in the back."

He couldn't help the grin that came over his face as he motioned his head to the back of the building. Next to him, Twan was shaking his head. Mac's eyes traveled up and down Erica's tight body, and when he got back to her face, she had a cute attitude going on that made him smile harder.

"I mean, if you can throw me in a little sack of something nice, we might can work somethin' out," Erica said, batting her lashes and rubbing Mac's chest with her freshly manicured nails.

The way she bit her bottom lip at him was enough to give any man an erection. Mac's high didn't make it any better. Everything he wanted to do to Erica was easily read on his face. Next to her, a jittery LuLu didn't seem to care what she had to do, as long as Erica got her drugs. Mac looked over at Twan, who waved him off. He already knew what time it was.

"I'ma be right back," Mac said, and the two men slapped hands.

"Aye," Twan said, pulling Mac close so he could speak to him in a low tone. "Strap up, motherfucka. She fuckin' for some powder. Ain't no tellin what else she done fucked for."

"Motherfucka, I know what I'm doin'," Mac said with a laugh.

"A'ight," Twan let his hand go and shrugged. "If you itchin' next week, don't say shit to me about it."

"The fuck you tryin'a say?" Erica snapped at him and turned up her nose in an offended fashion.

"Man, don't pay him no mind. Come on, baby. Show me what that mouth do," Mac said, taking her hand.

The annoyed look on her face faded, replaced by a sensual smile. As she let him guide her into Kent's, she flicked off Twan. LuLu stayed in the front, and Erica followed closely behind Mac. The store was cold, and Mac looked over at Kent, an older Black man and the store's owner. He was standing behind a glass window, serving people inside who were buying liquor and wraps for their weed.

"Aye, Kent," Mac called, and Kent looked up. "Let me back."

Mac motioned his hand toward the back door. Kent took one look at Erica and grinned. He handed the young man in front of him his change and then reached under the cash register. A door in the very back of the store took Mac and Erica outside again. The back of the store had a parking lot enclosed by a metal fence about six feet tall, with a gate leading to the street. A few vehicles were parked there, but Mac took her to the shiny black Escalade on rims.

"This your whip?" Erica asked in an impressed tone.

"I wouldn't be 'bout to fuck you in it if it wasn't," Mac said and opened the passenger door for her.

She giggled, and he helped her up into the seat. He stood in front of her, and she opened her legs so he could come closer. His hands found their way on the side of her thighs under her skirt and worked their way up her soft skin until they were under her soft butt. Back when he was growing up, a woman like Erica would have been far out of his league. Mac had never been the one girls looked at out of his crew. Most didn't go for the big Black guy with his strong features. They wanted the pretty boys. But he stopped having that problem the moment he started making real money in the streets. It was then that he realized women didn't see looks. They saw the clothes, cars and jewelry. They saw dollar signs, and as long as they were everywhere on him, Mac didn't have an issue anymore getting whatever woman he wanted.

"Why you looking at me like that?" Erica asked.

"'Cause a woman like you shouldn't have to do nothin' like this to get what she wants," he told her, and she laughed.

"I was raised to use what I got to get what I want," she said, running a finger down his lips. "And right now, I want what you got."

"You got somethin' I want too. And if it's good, we might can keep this up. What you think? Maybe we can go shoppin' or somethin'. It's a reason the pussy is shaped like a wallet, and I know that."

Erica grinned at the word "shopping." Mac knew he was going to get her with that one. Women loved to shop, and he didn't mind spending as long as they didn't mind fucking. Mac forced her legs open more, and Erica naturally leaned back, exposing the fact that she didn't have on any panties. Barely a millisecond passed before he dove in face-first. While he devoured her cat, pleasured moans began filling the air, intertwining with the sounds already in the night air. One could have assumed the noises were Erica's since her head was back and she was enjoying the experience. However, the loud moans belonged to Mac.

He was so loud, high and lost in the sauce that Erica didn't even need to squeeze her thighs over his ears to mask the sound of the fence shaking due to someone climbing it. Or the footsteps rushing toward them. However, when the guns cocked behind his head, he stopped everything he was doing midlick.

"I knew some pussy would be the downfall of yo' ugly ass," a rough voice said behind him.

Before he could turn around and see who it was, he was struck across the back of his head with the gun. It was enough to send him crashing to the ground, but not enough to knock him out. He looked up to see two masked men standing over him. One of them handed Erica some money after she hopped out of the car.

"Y-you set me up, bitch?" a discombobulated Mac said, trying to get back on his feet.

"They paid me a rack and said I could keep whatever powder you got on you," Erica said with a laugh, pulling down her skirt. "Plus, I got some head in the process. A win is a win."

Mac drew his own weapon and tried to lunge at her, but a powerful blow to the temple by one of the men put him down again. His gun went sliding across the ground. That time, when he fell, he felt himself growing faint. One of the men advanced on him, but he was too disoriented to do anything.

"Who are you?" he asked, watching the man pull a white towel from his back pocket.

"The Boogeyman, motherfucka," the man said and put the towel over Mac's face. Within seconds, Mac's body went limp. He was out cold.

Chapter 16

Business was buzzing that night, and Twan found himself losing track of time. He was serving customers left and right with whatever they needed. He had gotten so busy outside of Kent's that he hadn't even noticed that Mac hadn't come back yet. However, when he did, he stepped into the corner store to see if Mac might be there. His head did a few swivels around, but he didn't see Mac or Erica anywhere in sight.

"Kent," he said loudly to the store owner, who turned his head to the front entrance. "Mac in here?"

"Nah," Kent answered in a raspy voice and pointed at the back of the store. "Took shawty out there and ain't been back inside since. Maybe he left."

"Aye, buzz me back," Twan said and headed for the back door.

What he noticed when he got there was that he hadn't even needed Kent to buzz him back because there was a little rock holding the door partially open. He figured Mac must have done it so he could get back inside. He pushed it all the way open and looked outside, half expecting Mac to have Erica bent over and going to work. But the only thing he saw back there was his own car parked alongside Kent's. Mac and his truck were nowhere to be found. Twan smacked his lips and turned around. He couldn't believe Mac was missing out on the night's money for a random girl.

He walked back through the building and resumed his post. However, as he did so, he turned to face LuLu, who was sitting on the sidewalk in front of the store, waiting patiently for her niece to return with her goods.

"Ya ho-ass niece is gone, so you need to step too," he said to her and waved his hand in a shooing motion. LuLu was busy looking around the parking lot and chewing her lips to hear him. "Aye, LuLu, you ain't hear what I said? Ya niece didn't get shit for you. She gone."

"That girl wouldn't leave me," LuLu glared at him.

"Well, she did, so beat it. I got shit to do." He waved her off again.

"I'm not goin' nowhere until I get my shit. Like I said, she wouldn't leave me, and plus, there her car go right there. She drove me up here." She pointed down the street. "See, right there, behind that truck."

Twan squinted in the direction she pointed and saw what she was talking about. There was barely any light hitting that spot, but he was able to make out a silver car and a truck that resembled Mac's Escalade. He was too far away to tell for sure if it was Mac's truck, but when LuLu jumped up and went in that direction, something told him to follow her.

"He musta pulled around from the back," he said.

"I don't care what the fuck he did as long as he got my shit," LuLu said and put an extra pep in her step.

There were no lights on in either vehicle, nor was there any music playing. When LuLu got to it, she knocked on the tinted window quickly to get their attention. She stepped back when the driver's door opened, and Erica hopped out. Seeing that, Twan twisted up his mouth.

"Why you in the driver seat?" Twan asked. "Where Mac?"

The words had barely left his lips when the back door of the Escalade swung open, and a masked man hopped out with a gun pointed at his head. He reached for the gun on Twan's hip and snatched it. They were a good distance from the corner store, and the music was so loud over there that even if he shouted, no one would hear, or they would probably have thought he was a partier having a good time.

"Hands up, bitch," the masked man ordered, and Twan felt he didn't have a choice.

He knew then that Mac was either shot somewhere or dead. He gave Erica a chilling look, knowing she had constructed the whole robbery. She returned it with a sweet smile of her own. The man pressed the gun on Twan's temple, but he didn't flinch. It wasn't the first time he'd been in this predicament. However, he didn't want that night to be his last night breathing, either.

"Look, all I got on me is my jewelry and the money I made tonight. You can have it all. You don't gotta shoot me."

"Shut up," the man said, jerking the gun. "You ain't callin' no shots. I want the other money."

"What other money?" Twan asked, genuinely confused. "Only other thing I got is what I ain't sell tonight."

"You know what other money I'm talkin' about. The money you stole from Rome."

On the last word, the passenger-side door of the Escalade opened, and someone got out. Slowly, they made their way around the front end of the vehicle, and Twan's blood ran cold when they came into the light. Rome walked right toward him in all black and no mask. Twan understood then that this wasn't a petty robbery. It was the perfect setup. When Rome stopped in front of him, he turned his head to face LuLu.

"I don't think I'ma need you on the streets no more after this, Lu," Rome told her.

"Good. Because I was gettin' real tired of clockin' in as a crackhead every day," LuLu said in an even voice that didn't sound like the one Twan knew.

He watched in astonishment as right before his eyes, LuLu stood up straighter, licked the dryness from her lips and removed the tattered gray wig from her head, revealing short black locs. Twan's eyes widened as he tried to make sense of what was happening.

"What the fuck. You ain't a fiend? And you . . . ain't old?" His confusion made Rome chuckle.

"You thought I wouldn't have eyes on y'all's whole operation? Lu been workin' for me the whole time y'all been sellin' to her. She reports everything she sees back to me. And she ain't the only one. Now . . . Mac is on his way to somewhere nobody will ever find 'im, and do you know what I'm about to do to his fat ass?"

"You about to kill him."

"Not right away, nah. But he gon' have a real long night if he don't tell me everything I need to know, especially about the location of where my fuckin' money is. And so are you."

He made a gesture with his hand, and before Twan could react, he felt the gun come crashing down on his head. The blow was followed by searing pain, causing him to fall to the ground. His eyesight instantly went hazy, blood trickling down his face. His consciousness was fading, but he guessed they wanted to make sure he was out for the count. Before he knew it, the gun came crashing down in the exact same place . . . and everything went quiet.

Chapter 17

Although it was late, Pea was wide awake. It was going to be a long night, and she knew it the moment she saw Rome walk out wearing all black. She had flashbacks of her own brothers going on missions her grandfather sent them on, and usually "all black" meant someone was going to die. She trusted Rome to make it home safely, but, like a mother or an aunt, she worried and wouldn't stop until she saw him walk through the front door in one piece. When he did, she knew it was her job to get rid of every article of clothing he was wearing and scrub the house top to bottom.

She sat in the dimly lit kitchen at the island with a bottle of wine, watching reruns of her favorite show on the television on the counter. She would have invited Draya to join her, but she didn't for two reasons, and one of them was that she wasn't there to begin with. The clock was pushing midnight, and although Pea knew she'd gone to a comedy show, it should have been over by then. No sooner had she taken a few more sips of her wine than she heard a key turn and the front door open.

"Hello?" she heard Draya call from the foyer of the house. "Is anybody home?"

Pea didn't say anything. However, when she heard Draya stumbling around trying to make her way through the house, she turned her head just in time to see her make it to the kitchen. Pea couldn't help but let out an annoyed breath at the sight of her. She was clearly drunk, and her hair was disheveled. She had one heel on, and the other was hanging around her ankle, as if she had tried to take it off but failed. But despite her appearance, she had a big smile on her face and was in a fit of giggles. Pea got up and helped her over to the island and up on a chair.

"I don't need your help," Draya said through her giggles and tried to snatch away from her.

"Girl, clearly you do. You must have had a great time at the show," Pea said, removing Draya's shoes.

"It was fantastic. I haven't laughed that hard in so long," Draya said, smiling. She looked around. "Where's Rome?"

"He's still out."

"Of course, he is. You know, for once, I'd like . . . I'd like to know w-what it feels like to have my boyfriend trip on me for coming in late. I guess I'll never know because his ass is always gone."

"You know what Rome does to take care of his family. He's home enough, and you should appreciate that," Pea said blandly after dropping the shoes on the ground and sitting back in her seat.

She went back to sipping her wine and planned to listen to Draya complain about Rome not being home for what felt like the millionth time. That was one of the reasons the two of them couldn't get along. Any chance Draya got, she was always complaining about something. She was insatiable. It seemed that nothing Rome did made her happy. Even knowing everything he was going through at the moment, and still making everything about her, just added to Pea's displeasure.

"I want to be a priority—not an option. He promised he'd go to the comedy show with me. And instead, he's out in the streets . . . again."

"You *do* remember y'all got shot at, *right?* He's out there making sure it doesn't happen again."

"You know . . . You know what h-he promised me earlier today?" she slurred. "He promised me he was gonna go legit. But I know he was just sayin' that to get some pussy. That boy ain't never leaving these streets alone."

"You don't know that. I think he's gonna be out of them real soon," Pea told her.

"Yeah? How do you know?" Draya asked, and when she tried to reach for the bottle of wine, Pea snatched it away and cut her eyes at her.

"We both know why," Pea told her. "And you're lucky I don't whoop your ass for drinkin' like you clearly have been tonight."

"I don't know what you're talking about," Draya said, averting her eyes.

"You don't? Well, let me tell you. You complain about Rome not doing enough for you. That man doesn't make you lift a finger in this house. Hell, it should be you burning his clothes and cleaning this house top to bottom after he finishes what needs to be done. But no, that's my job. And you know what else my job is? Keeping this home stocked with everything it needs, including *your* toiletries and sanitation products."

"You're just talking, Pea. I'm going to bed." Draya made to get up, but Pea grabbed her by her arm.

"No, I'm talking about that box of tampons I bought you three months ago and how it's in the exact same place I put it—untouched."

"Okay, I bought my own this time. So?"

"You *do* know I'm the one that changes the trash too. I ain't seen a tampon or a pad in months. You're pregnant, aren't you?"

Pea thought Draya was going to deny it. She thought she was going to snatch away and run as fast as her drunk legs would take her. But suddenly, all the fun she had that night faded from her face, and she began to bawl, crying hard. Her body went limp, and she fell into Pea's shoulder, her body shaking with each sob. Pea instantly wrapped her arms around her and let the girl get it all out. By the time Draya got control of herself and pulled away, the shoulder of Pea's robe was drenched in tears, spit and snot. Pea got up to get her a paper towel to wipe her face.

"You can't tell him. I can't have this baby," Draya said when she took the paper towel.

"Why can't you?" Pea asked, standing in front of her. She forced Draya to look at her. "You love him, don't you?"

"Yeah, I do. But he don't love me. Not enough. And I can't bring a baby into a world where all the love that's owed to me will skip me and go right to them. That's not fair to me. *I'm* the one who's been here."

"So, you don't want to have the baby because you think Rome will love them more than you?"

"You just said it. And that was all I needed to know," Draya said, looking at Pea with tearful eyes. "He'll get out of the game for sure for a person we don't even know. But not for me. Not *just* for me."

"That's so selfish."

"And I don't give a fuck. I know what I want is out there, and if Rome can't give it to me, I can't give him this child," Draya said, getting up and pushing Pea out of the way.

"Please think about what you're saying. Don't get rid of that baby. Rome does love you, more than you'll ever know. That baby you're carrying is a blessing, and you need to take better care of yourself. You know Rome will be a good father," Pea said to Draya's back as she walked away.

Draya stopped in her tracks, and Pea thought that maybe something she said might have gotten through to her. However, when the girl whipped around and looked at her with angry, fiery eyes, she knew nothing had.

"I don't know shit but the fact that you better keep this between us. If not, you'll regret it."

Draya's tone was so frigid that it actually gave Pea chills crawling down her spine. Not because she was afraid, but because she genuinely didn't know what to do. She wanted to respect Draya's wishes, woman to woman. But if Rome ever found out that she knew about Draya being pregnant and she got an abortion, he'd never trust or forgive her again. All she could do right then was let Draya walk away and hope for the best.

Chapter 18

The sound of glass shattering made 15-year-old Slaw's eyes open. He had been sound asleep in the twin bed in his bedroom. Although his door was shut, his ears were filled with loud shouting coming from the living room of the apartment he shared with his mother. He heard two voices, one he recognized as his mom's and the other belonged to her ex-boyfriend, Gary. Slaw hated him, mainly for the way he treated his mom. They'd been together for a year and had an abusive relationship. Gary was a mean, nasty drunk, and the abuse had caused the relationship Slaw had with his mother to be strained. He was tired of seeing it. But his mom had finally gotten tired of the constant fighting and had kicked Gary to the curb a week ago. Things had been peaceful up until that point, and Slaw had been getting along better with his mom.

"You're a whore!"

"Baby, no. No, I love you. I just needed a break away from this. I—"

"Shut the fuck up!"

Hearing Gary's angry voice as he shouted at the top of his lungs and the terrified tone of his mother's made Slaw hop out of bed. He swung open his bedroom door and ran to the living room in nothing but a pair of shorts and a T-shirt. Once there, he took in the scene at hand. His mom was a very meticulous woman. Nothing was ever out of place in her home. But right then, it looked like a tornado had passed through the house. Photos had been knocked off the wall, one of the dining room chairs had been shattered and the couches had been completely shifted. His eyes fell on his mother, and he was mortified to see one of her eyes swollen shut, along with blood leaking from her nose. She was cowering in a corner with her arms up as if to protect herself from any further blows.

"I know you been seeing another man, Tali. Everybody at the bar told me they saw you out with Harold," he bellowed as he towered over her.

"Harold and me are just friends, Gary! Please stop."

"Bitch, I'ma kill you," Gary shouted and hauled back to hit her again.

Before he could lay another hand on her, Slaw ran up on him and shoved him hard to the side. Gary stumbled away and fell. But he quickly stood straight again and glared at Slaw as the boy positioned himself between Gary and his mom. Gary was a few inches taller than Slaw, but Slaw wasn't a little guy by any means. Still, seeing the teenager there to defend his mother didn't put any fear in Gary at all.

"The fuck you gon' do to me, li'l motherfucka? This here is between me and ya mom."

"I'ma give you one chance to walk," Slaw warned him and pointed at the door.

Gary followed Slaw's finger with his eyes and laughed. Then he turned his attention back to Slaw and took a few steps toward them. The closer he got, the more Slaw could smell the liquor seeping from his pores. His mustache and beard were messy, and his clothes looked filthy, like he'd been at the bar for days straight.

"And like I said, what you gon' do if I don't? Huh?" Gary asked, still advancing on Slaw.

When he was directly in front of him, Gary pushed Slaw back by his chest. Slaw knocked his hands away, but Gary pushed him again . . . and again—each time with more force. When Slaw tried to swing, Gary blocked it and struck him in the jaw. Slaw went flying back into his mother, who screamed.

"Slaw, go back to your room, baby. I'll handle this," his mom urged, trying to push Gary away so he wouldn't hit Slaw again.

"Handle what, bitch?" Gary asked and backhanded her as hard as he could.

Seeing his helpless mother get swatted like a fly ignited a fire inside of Slaw that he didn't know was there. He jumped to his feet and began laying heavy hits into Gary, catching the man off guard. Slaw saw his fists swinging, but he was numb to them landing. Then he saw blood coming from Gary's face. He had completely zoned out and didn't stop beating Gary, even when his mother was screaming at him to stop. The beating only ended when Gary dropped to the ground from the final blow to the head that Slaw served him.

Slaw blinked and felt tension leaving his body. He was breathing heavily, and his fists were bloody. On the ground, Gary was barely conscious, and to Slaw's surprise, Tali ran to her abuser.

"Baby? Oh, honey, we need to get you some help," she said, dropping down beside him.

"He . . . He tried to kill m-me," Gary barely got out.

"W-what have you done?" Tali glared at her son with tears streaming down her face. She began tenderly cradling Gary's head against her chest. "What have you done?"

"Mama, he was hurting you. I—"

"I told you to go to your room. Now, you've almost killed him!"

"Mama—"

" Get out," she said icily.

"What?"

"Get. Out."

"O-okay, I'll go to my room," Slaw said, backing away, but then his mom looked up and glared at him.

"No. I can't . . . I can't live like this. There can't be two thinking they're the man of this house. You need to find somewhere else to go, Slaw."

Her words cut deeper than a dagger to his heart. He searched her face for any sign of empathy, but there was none. She stared at him with disgust.

"Mama, you choosing this drunk over me? Your son?"

"You're old enough to make it on your own. You're part of the reason we get into it so much. A boy your age should be bringing some more money into this house. I know what you do in them streets."

"I'm not the parent. I'm tryin'a save up so I can get up out of here," Slaw told her.

"And while you're thinking about you, I need to think about me. I've done all I can for you. I just wanna live my own life," she said, looking into his eyes. "This can't happen again. I love him, and I can't have you challenging him in his own house."

"His *house?"*

"Just go. Please, just leave. Look at what you've done to him," she said, sobbing over Gary.

Slaw was truly sickened by the sight. Even if she were to come to her senses, Slaw realized he wouldn't want to stay there anyway. He went to his bedroom and packed as many of his belongings as would fit into a duffel bag. The last thing he did was reach under his mattress and grab the 9-mm pistol he had for protection while he was in the streets. He walked out of the bedroom for the last time and headed for the front door. Before he left, he passed by where his mom was still cradling Gary and whispering sweet nothings to him. Slaw stopped beside them to look at his mother for a moment, and she looked up at him unapologetically. They had the same eyes. However, when she looked at him through hers, she couldn't have seen something she truly loved. He was disposable to her, and there were no words to describe the pain that came with that.

"Today is the day that my heart broke," Slaw told her flatly. "I think it's only fair that it be the same for you."

Before his mom could react, Slaw aimed the gun at Gary's head and pulled the trigger.

Slaw jerked back into the present day, waking up from the same dream he'd been having for years. Well, it wasn't a dream. It was a core memory. One that reminded him of his origin story. His nickname had been "Slaw" since he was a kid, because he was the only baby his grandmother had ever seen eat coleslaw. However, that was the night the monster in him was truly born. It was also the night that he took his first life.

He made to get up, but he felt a slight weight on his chest. When he looked down, he suddenly remembered where he was, on the living room couch of the apartment he stayed in part time with Milla. Sleeping peacefully on him was his young son, Cairo. The boy was the spitting image of Slaw. He couldn't deny him if he wanted to. He was one of two things in the world that brought Slaw joy. If it weren't for Cairo, Slaw might not have had any humanity left. He hadn't planned to have a child with Milla. She was the type of woman who pleased his sexual desires, not the kind that he would plan a life with. She thought that a baby would make him love her, but back then, he never thought he could love another woman after his experience with his mother. The biggest thing he didn't like about her was that she was weak. Her thirst for his returned affections would keep her loyal to him forever. However, he needed a woman who made him chase her. Who made him want her. Not someone who submitted for no reason. That reminded him too much of his mother.

A news story being played on the big-screen television in the living room caught his attention. The volume wasn't loud, but he could hear well enough. A young, blue-eyed, blond woman reported about a recent homicide with the photo of the victim on the screen. He was a scruffy-looking Black man who appeared to have lived a hard life.

"Officers responded to a complaint about a foul smell coming from a Buckhead apartment. When they arrived, they found Adam Barkley unresponsive after suffering a gunshot wound to the back of his head. They believe he was deceased in the apartment for over seventy-two hours. There are no known suspects at this time."

"Slaw?" He heard Milla's timid voice say.

He looked away from the TV to see her stepping out of the hallway shadows. The sun had gone down, so she was wearing a flowy teddy nightgown and a head scarf. Her eyes matched the sound of her voice, and she looked as if she were silently questioning approaching him. They hadn't said much to each other since the incident in the closet.

"What?" he asked, and she held up his throwaway phone in one of her hands.

"This keeps goin' off," she said.

Carefully sitting up so he wouldn't wake his son, Slaw reached for the phone and waited for Milla to bring it to him. When she did, he grabbed her hand before taking the device out of it. He held it for a moment, and hope flickered in her eyes. She took a shaky breath.

"Slaw, I—"

"Know what this is, and what it will always be, right?" Slaw asked, and saw the hope fade as quickly as it had come. "You're the mother of my son, but I can't give you me, do you understand that?"

"I do . . . but I'll never stop trying."

"Then you're going to keep breaking your own heart. The most I can give you is that money I left on the nightstand. I won't be staying over anymore either."

He watched her catch her breath and swallowed the lump in her throat. He knew what he was saying was killing her inside, especially since he hadn't broken eye contact once. But he didn't really care. She didn't say anything else. Instead, she pulled her hand away and left the phone in his. Before exiting, she took Cairo from his arms and went back to her bedroom.

Slaw sighed and wiped his hand down on his face. He saw that he had a few missed calls from Bizzy and one from an unknown number. He decided to call the unknown number first since he assumed it was Detective Bradshaw. If it was him, hopefully, he had some good words for him. The call rang twice before it was answered.

"About time you called me back. I have news for you," Detective Bradley's gruff voice said from the other end.

"Shit, I hope it's something I want to hear."

"It might be. Remember that witness I was telling you about? I found him. His name is Adam Barkley. Well, it was. I handled it," Detective Bradshaw said, and Slaw smirked.

"So that was your handiwork?"

"You must have seen the news. I gotta tell you, it wasn't easy. They had him holed away in a safe house, and I had to jump through a lot of hoops to find out where. That kind of takedown comes with an extra fee."

"How much we talkin'?" Slaw asked.

"Ten thousand."

"Done. I'll have it to you by the morning."

"Always nice doing business with you, Slaw," Detective Bradshaw said and disconnected the call.

"I bet, you slimy motherfucka," Slaw said to himself, scrolling in his call log and calling Bizzy's number.

"Damn, I been blowin' yo' ass up for the past few hours," Bizzy said from the other end of the phone when he answered.

"Been with Cairo. And I just got off the phone with Bradshaw. That little problem we had got taken care of. It cost a nice piece, though. I'ma go to the stash and drop that off in the morning."

"Yeah . . . about that," Bizzy said hesitantly.

"About what?"

"You talk to Mac or Twan lately?" Bizzy asked, and Slaw racked his brain.

"Not in some days, no."

"Me either. And the motherfuckas ain't been answerin' the phone either. I stopped by Kent's, and they weren't at they usual post up. Talked to Kent, and he said last time he seen him was some nights ago. Said he went to the back of the store to fuck a bitch, but after that, he left. His truck was gone."

Slaw could see Mac taking a girl to the back for a quickie. The man was addicted to pussy. But it wasn't like him or Twan not to report in. It definitely wasn't like them to miss out on a moneymaking opportunity. Whatever was going on, there had better be a good reason for it.

"But that's not even the biggest problem," Bizzy continued. "You know the money we hit Rome for? It's gone. Well, fifty thousand of it."

"The fuck you mean the money gone?"

"Just like I said. It's gone. I checked the spot, and it ain't there."

"So, half my money is gone. You think Mac stole it?"

"Him and Twan the only other people who knew where it was. So, it don't take a rocket scientist to put two and two together."

Slaw felt his jaw clenching not only from the thought of being robbed by people he trusted, but also because he had been in the process of getting a new drug connect and putting together a life-changing play. The thing was, he needed that money to complete the transaction.

"Why the fuck would Mac steal from me? He eats good under me."

"I don't know. Maybe seeing how fast and the way you killed Vonte spooked him enough to take the money and run," Bizzy suggested. "Maybe he thought he was next, especially knowing that there was a witness that night. But I'm on the way to the main spot to check on the other half of the money."

"I'll meet you there."

Chapter 19

The only sound that could be heard when Slaw stepped out of his car was the crickets chirping in the night. Every hustler had a main spot that only their most trusted knew about, and Slaw's was located in a rural area on the outskirts of the city, sitting on a nice chunk of land. There were barely any streetlights, and the closest neighbors were a few miles up the road. The home had been passed down to him from his grandparents and was supposed to be used as a family home. Slaw, however, had turned it into an upscale trap-and-stash house, so it had seen its fair share of money, drugs and violence.

Bizzy was already there, and Slaw had parked behind his car. As he approached, he could see through the sidelights that the entryway lights were on in the house. The front door hadn't been closed all the way, and although sloppy, Slaw chalked it up to Bizzy knowing he was on the way. All he cared about was making sure his money was still in the safe inside.

He went inside, but he didn't get far once the door was closed behind him. He stopped in his tracks immediately at the sight of a blood streak leading down the wooden hallway floor to the kitchen. It looked as if someone had been injured badly and dragged away. Instinct led his hand to draw the gun on his waist and get into a defensive stance. He steadied his breathing and listened for any sign of life in the house.

"Bizzy?" he said, hoping he'd hear the familiar voice of his partner talk back. "Bizzy?"

The second time he said Bizzy's name, he spoke a little louder. However, still nothing. He slowly started making his way deeper inside the house, pointing his gun into every room he passed. The house was radio silent, and that made the hair on the back of his neck stand up. He continued toward the kitchen, where the only light came from a bulb above the stove. When he got there, his eyes instantly went to the wooden dining room table where he could clearly see Bizzy sitting. He didn't understand why he hadn't answered when he called if he was just in the kitchen.

"Bizzy? Why didn't you say nothing when I just called you?" he asked, lowering his gun and going to the table. Bizzy still didn't say anything. "Bizzy? You hear me talking to you. Where that blood come from in the front?"

He shook Bizzy's shoulder to get an answer, but was stunned when Bizzy's body lifelessly toppled over. When it did, he was able to see a huge, gaping hole in the back of his head oozing blood. He was dead. He didn't have time to process it before the lights flipped on.

"Psst," he heard a loud whisper on his right side just before someone launched an attack on him.

Slaw was easily able to dodge the first punch, but when he raised his gun and turned to face his attacker, his weapon was knocked out of his hand. A fist crashed into his face, sending him stumbling back. He caught himself before he fell on the floor and looked up at who was fighting him.

"Rome," he growled, seeing his enemy standing a few feet away.

Rome was dressed in nice gear, head to toe, his large "C" pendant on his thick chain shining in the light. He would be considered fresh if it weren't for the blood all over his jersey and his jeans. Slaw spat the blood in his mouth out on the floor and wiped the corner of his mouth with the back of his hand. His eyes darted to the gun that wasn't too far from his feet, but the sound of a gun cocking stopped him.

"I wouldn't do that if I were you," a different male voice said.

From where he stood, Slaw turned his head to the left and saw Rome's little brother, Dru, standing in an entranceway that led to one of the hallways of the home. He too had blood on his clothing. It looked as if they'd gone on a murderous binge. He held a gun in his right hand pointed at Slaw. Also hanging from his right shoulder was a black duffel bag, which Slaw assumed was filled with the money he stole. Slaw knew that going for the pistol was a bad idea. Dru wouldn't hesitate to blow him away. Instead, he went back to glaring at Rome. It seemed like their game of chess had abruptly ended. Slaw hadn't even been able to make all the moves he wanted to yet.

"So, this how it's going to end, huh?" he asked.

"What do you think? You killed my people, stole from me and sent some motherfuckas to shoot at my family," Rome said.

"I also infiltrated your organization in the best way. How do you think I knew where the money was going to be in the first place? And what about Clem and Shun . . . Do you think everyone around you is loyal? They proved to be flawed. You don't know who else is waiting on them tables to turn," Slaw taunted, but Rome's face didn't change.

"Always gon' be a snake somewhere when this type of money is comin' in. I'll weed 'em out eventually," Rome shrugged. "But I'ma still have an organization. Yours dies today. What you thought I was gon' do? Play ring-around-the-rosy like you? Nah, I'm a *real* boss. I do house calls. Courtesy of your boys, of course."

He made a gesture to Dru, who used his free hand to reach into the duffel bag on his shoulder. Slaw thought they were going to rub taking the money back in his face, but that wasn't what was in the bag at all. Dru tossed two things at Slaw's feet, and when he looked, he saw they were two severed heads: Mac's and Twan's, to be exact.

"Of course, it took a little persuadin', but in the end, they told us everything we needed to know about you and ya operation. We figured it was only a matter of time before y'all came here, especially after you found out we took my money back," Rome smirked. "But even if you didn't show up here, I know how to draw you out. That condo in Midtown? You know, the one you be playin' family man in? I would love to meet little Cairo."

At the mention of his son, Slaw lurched for Rome. He didn't care that there was a gun pointed at him. Rome knew what he was doing. Off to the side, Dru didn't lower his weapon, but he didn't shoot either. Instead, he let his brother enjoy a victory that Slaw wouldn't yet accept.

Rome had his fists up before Slaw threw his first jab. Rome blocked it and sent one flying back. Slaw ducked, already knowing what kind of power Rome's blows contained, and hit Rome in the ribs. He heard Rome groan and thought he had done enough damage to hit him with an uppercut, but Rome sidestepped him and caught him in his jaw. Rome didn't give Slaw time to recover. He stepped forward and began walking him down with his fists. Slaw tried to fight back. He even landed a few more hits, but Rome was just too strong.

"Whoop him, Ro. Whoop that motherfucka," Dru cheered fiercely from the sidelines.

Blood trickled into Slaw's eyes, blurring his vision, and he couldn't block Rome's attacks. However, Slaw would never forget the hatred in Rome's eyes. Slaw felt the life leaving his body, along with all his energy. He was convinced Rome was about to kill him with his bare hands. The last punch to Slaw's temple completely disconcerted him. He fell to the ground, breathing like a dog left out in the sun too long. He was seeing double. Two Romes stood over him, also breathing heavily, and flexing their muscles.

"I also meant to tell you, Mac told us where your stash spots were too," Rome said, catching his own breath. "Everybody in 'em dead. All your drugs are here, all your money is too. I'm not like you. I can make my own pape. So, all your shit? Everything you've ever worked for? It all dies with you."

Slaw watched him step away for a brief moment before coming back. When he did, he began tossing some liquid on him. It felt cold like water, but Slaw could recognize the smell of gasoline. Rome and Dru began dousing the whole home, and while they were doing that, Slaw's eyes went from Bizzy's dead body to the two severed heads on the ground. He didn't want to die like them, but if it were inevitable, he didn't want anyone to make it out. His gaze fell on the gun he'd dropped earlier, and although his body seared in pain, he willed all his last strength up and out. He dragged his battered body across the gasoline-soaked kitchen floor toward the gun. When he was close enough to grab it, he reached his hand out, but the second he touched it, a foot plowed into his already bloody face. Slaw groaned loudly and rolled on his back.

"Didn't I tell you not to try it?" Dru's annoyed voice sounded, and he kicked the gun far away.

"You shoulda stayed in yo' lane, Slaw. Motherfuckas like you . . . Enough ain't never enough. Maybe I'll see you in hell, or maybe I'll change my life." Rome stood over Slaw once more, holding a box of matches in his hands. "Either way, I don't wanna go out like this or like you. Let's go, Dru."

Slaw heard their footsteps walk to the front of the house and the front door open, but it didn't close. Slaw didn't need two guesses why. Moments later, he heard a loud "*whoosh,*" followed by rapid crackling as a fire spread. It quickly escalated to a roar as the flames intensified. Windows in the living room shattered from the heat. Slaw could see the smoke and knew it would be seconds before the fire consumed everything in its path, including him. As the flames closed in on him, he shut his eyes as his thoughts went to the one thing that had mattered to him in the game. What it would have felt like to be king.

Chapter 20

"Happy Birthday, dear Nami. Happy Birthday to you. . . ."

The large crowd of people singing was deafening as they wished Nami a happy twentieth birthday. She stood, beaming, in the center of the large social hall, surrounded by all her loved ones. Everyone was dressed to impress, and Nami herself was wearing a shimmery, gold minidress. She rocked pin curls and a long side bang with a spiral at the end. Nami was easily stealing the show and enjoying every second of it. Balloons in shades of gold, pink and white cascaded from the ceiling, catching the light and casting a festive glow across the room. The tables and chairs had been decorated to match the color scheme, and every seat was filled.

To the side, a long table almost groaned under the weight of a delectable spread of fried chicken, smothered pork chops, oxtails, cabbage, collard greens, macaroni and cheese and many more pans of delectable food. Aromas of the savory spices and sweet treats wafted through the air. Almost everyone had gotten themselves a plate. A DJ in the corner briefly stopped playing their jams so everyone could sing "Happy Birthday." Rome and Dru stood in front of Nami, singing the loudest. A part of that might have had to do with the spiked punch they were both sipping on in their red cups. Aunt Malia wasn't too far from everybody, taking photos on her camera, all smiles. Draya stood behind them, shaking her head at their unapologetic tipsiness. Beside Nami,

Jelia and Pea stood holding a two-tier marble cake. It had white frosting with strawberries around both tiers and a strawberry-flavored drizzle. Nami closed her eyes for a few moments before blowing out the lit number 20 candle on top of the cake. Everyone cheered, and a strong pair of arms wrapped around her. She beamed when she looked over her shoulder and saw Jyair. She'd never been happier in her whole life.

"Put ya fuckin' cups up for my baby sister!" Rome's voice boomed, and everyone did as they were told.

It had been almost three months since he killed Slaw. Now, he wanted to do something special for his sister. A celebration was what everyone needed after so much bloodshed and all the losses. So many families were still grieving, not to mention the loss of Old Lamont, which continued to shake the community. However, slowly but surely, things were going back to normal. Or a new normal anyway. Rome looked lovingly down at Nami, and she returned it with her gaze.

"I wanna wish you the happiest birthday and say congratulations on gettin' ya cosmetology license and openin' ya own shop. You doin' it, baby girl, and I'm so proud of you. Prouder than our father coulda ever been," he told her, and Nami brushed tears from the corner of her eyes. "I remember when Mama brought you home from the hospital. You were so small. Me and Dru ain't even wanna touch you 'cause we ain't think you was real."

"Yeah, but we figured that shit out quick 'cause all you did was cry," Dru jumped in, and everyone laughed.

"You been spoiled since the beginnin'," Rome smiled.

"And whose fault is that?" Nami put her hand on her hip and rolled her neck.

"A'ight, you got me there. You just always been so sweet. So beautiful . . . I remember wonderin' how I was gon' let you go? I ain't even wanna think about one of these suckas out here doin' you bad. I guess Jyair ain't too bad of a choice, though."

The crowd laughed again. It had never been a secret to him that Nami had a crush on Jyair, and he knew that it was only out of respect for Rome that Jyair never tried to get at her. But he would have had to be blind not to see how the man looked at his sister. He never saw an ounce of lust; always awe. Rome knew there was a chance that they would grow closer when he put Jyair in charge of Nami's safety during the feud with Slaw. What he didn't know was that the two would fall in love.

"Shit, you know she forever safe with me, Ro. One day, we gon' all be real brothers 'cause this girl gon' be my wife. I love her," Jyair said earnestly.

"Aw, baby, I love you too." Nami looked over her shoulder, and the two exchanged a quick kiss in front of everyone.

"Just make sure that ring is on her finger before y'all think about havin' babies," Jelia said, raising her brows at the couple.

"Mama, ain't nobody thinkin' 'bout no babies. Plus, twins run in Jy's family. I am *not* tryin'a lose my figure to no kids I don't even know," Nami said seriously.

"Mm-hmm. Well, we are about to go cut this damn cake for anyone who wants some, even though we really don't need any more desserts on that table," she said.

"Heck, we don't need any more food, period. But Rome insisted we go all out."

"Only the best for the best," Rome said, motioning for the DJ to start playing again.

Once the music started booming from the speakers, everyone felt compelled to hit the dance floor. A fine thing pulled Dru out on it, and they began grinding to the beat. Nami and Jyair, of course, were in the mix, having the time of their lives. Rome turned to Draya and grabbed her hands, trying to pull her out.

"Come on, baby, let's go dance," Rome said, but Draya looked at the crowded dance floor and shook her head.

"No, I think I'm just gonna sit down for a second."

"What? Girl, you love to dance. You just insecure 'cause you put on a little weight," Rome teased.

Draya's body had always been snatched, but lately, she'd been eating more, and it was showing. Typically, for a party like this, she would have been in something that showed off as much skin as possible, but this night she was wearing a loose-fitting maxi dress. He wanted her to know he didn't care, and that he liked the weight on her. She'd always been beautiful to him. She, however, didn't take lightly to his joke and snatched her hands out of his.

"Forget you, Rome." Before she could walk away, he grabbed her again and wrapped his arms around her shoulders from behind.

"My bad, baby," he said in her ear, swaying back and forth to the music. "You been tense all night, though. What's wrong?"

"Nothing, I just don't wanna dance. Damn, is that a crime?"

"Nah, but you not tellin' me what the real issue is."

"You know what the issue is. It's the same as it always is," she said, and he sighed.

"Baby, I don't know how many more times you want me to apologize, but here's another one. I'm sorry. I know shit ain't been what you wanted the last few months, but I just need a little more time to set up some shit and get out of the game."

"You've said that already, Rome. How much more time do you need? I can't keep doing this."

"Don't say that to me," Rome said, spinning her around and lifting her head by her chin. "I love you. It's gon' be you and me forever. And I know it's Nami's birthday, but

I know you been havin' an attitude with me, so meet me in the parking garage in half an hour."

"For what?"

"Just come outside in thirty minutes, okay? Ten o'clock. Be there. But for now, let me party with my sister one last time before she get too lost in her new life."

He leaned down and kissed Draya, and she reluctantly kissed him back. He paid it no mind, though. He let her go, and his face turned up into a smile as he went to join his siblings on the dance floor. Draya would come around, especially when she saw the gift he got her. Not only that, but he had been telling the truth when he said that he was close to getting out of the game and going completely legit. He thought the last batch would have been his last flip, but the effect of what Slaw had done was much heavier than he thought. He had to restructure his whole business and move more slowly, not faster, as he wanted. Rome never wanted to be in a position where something could get as close to destroying everything he built again. Not only that, but also Slaw's last words played over and over in his head.

"You don't know who else is waiting on them tables to turn."

He believed what Slaw said, and because of that, he no longer trusted anyone except for his family. If those tables did turn, Rome planned to be long gone from the game before it happened. Maybe even move to a different city and start a new life. However, when he moved to the center of the dance floor, completely stealing the show, and his siblings came to challenge his moves, he knew he wanted to enjoy the one he still had.

Chapter 21

From the sidelines, Draya texted on her phone and watched as Rome had a good time at the party. There wasn't a Debbie Downer in sight, as everyone wore smiles. But why wouldn't they when they were partying with the kingpin and had what seemed like unlimited food and drinks? Draya was the only one who was not enjoying herself. She was ready for the night to end.

The growing baby in her stomach had been making it harder and harder each day to contain her emotions. She didn't understand how he had time to coordinate such an extravagant party for Nami, but had never done anything so grand for her. Jealousy was feasting away at her, and she was doing nothing to stop it. Holding her stomach, she glared at them all, feeling completely out of place.

Recently, she'd been asking herself why she had stayed so long in the first place. Of course, she seemed happy on the surface, but the truth was, she hadn't been happy for a long time. Not even when Rome made her laugh, or when she did get a little of his time. The only time she ever felt a smidge of what she did when they first met was when Rome made her orgasm. She would never deny that the man had good sex, but even that didn't mean anything to her anymore because she knew things would go back to their standard settings once the lovemaking was over.

She had meant what she said when she told Pea she didn't want to have a baby with Rome. Thoughts of being stuck alone in a house with Pea and a baby day in and day out plagued her mind. Most women would have called her crazy or ungrateful. Rome provided her with everything most girls could want. And while Draya would never say she didn't love the material things and financial freedom Rome offered, she needed attention and to be watered like a flower. She felt there was no guarantee that, when Rome became who he wanted to be, he would be who she needed him to be. Or if he would even still want her. He didn't even know her anymore. That was why she had to do what she had to do, and that was look out for herself.

"I'm sorry, little baby," she said to her stomach after sending one last message and tucking her phone away in her purse.

She was happy that she'd always taken care of her body, because even at five months, her baby bump was barely showing. Of course, she'd gained a little weight, but she just attributed it to her eating more. It was easy to hide the pregnancy from Rome since he was always off somewhere, handling business or catching up on sleep when he *was* home. And when he tried to have sex recently, she would say she was on her cycle or act like she had an attitude, even though it wasn't really an act. She was sick and tired.

Speaking of sick and tired, the loud music, mixed with the beat's vibrations, nauseated her. She'd been trying to hold off until closer to the time Rome told her to meet her out front, but if she stood there much longer, she was going to throw up everything she'd eaten that day. Turning away from the dance floor with a slight stank face, Draya made her way out of the main floor of the social hall and headed to the kitchen area. She'd seen Pea leave with the rest of the cake that couldn't fit on the table, and Draya assumed she took it to the kitchen with the rest of the extra food. She moved quickly, trying to gather her emotions and her wits.

As she neared the big, stainless steel double doors of the kitchen, she could see Pea moving around through the two square windows on them. Nervousness overcame Draya just as the nausea had a few moments ago. She took a few deep breaths before pushing through the doors. When she did, she was hit with a wave of warmth and the smell of industrial cleaner mixed with food. Pea was wearing an apron over her dress and seemed to be in the middle of getting ahead on cleaning, so she wouldn't have much work to do at the end of the party. She stood over the sink spraying the loud sprayer. She hadn't even heard Draya enter behind her. When she finished rinsing off some champagne flutes, she turned to grab a stack of plates on a counter behind her.

"I don't know why the hell Rome insisted on real china instead of paper pl—oh!" She jumped when she saw Draya standing behind her. She put her hand to her chest. "Girl, you about scared the shit outta me, literally."

"I didn't mean to," was all Draya responded with, and Pea looked at her strangely.

"You okay? Did you need something?" Pea asked, but Draya was quiet for a moment. "Hellooo?"

"I just wanted to come talk to you about something," Draya said as she felt like the room was starting to close in on her.

"Hmmm . . . I'ma have to go get my own cleaning supplies from the car," Pea said to herself as she examined the food stuck to the plates on the counter. She glanced back up at Draya as she went over to where her purse hung on the wall and took out a set of car keys. "Okay, well, spit it out."

"It's about Rome," Draya said, and Pea rolled her eyes.

"Girl, we are at a party. I am not about to listen to you complain about him right now." Pea waved her hands in the air, causing her keys to jangle as she made her way to the kitchen doorway.

"It's not just Rome I want to talk about. It's the baby," Draya said. "I'm gonna keep him."

"Him?" Pea stopped in her tracks and whipped around. Her eyes were wide with excitement. "Oh my goodness, it's a boy? Oh my. I'm so happy. What made you change your mind?"

"I . . . I love him already. And I know he can love me. I want to give him a good life, a happy life."

"Rome is going to be so happy," Pea said, and fanned herself. "It's been killing me keeping this from him."

"That's the thing," Draya swallowed. "Rome can never know about the baby. Nobody can."

"What are you talking about?"

Pea's confused expression quickly turned to shock when Draya brandished a handgun from her purse. It was the same one Rome had given her months before. Pea froze when Draya aimed it at her.

"I'm sorry," Draya breathed and pulled the trigger.

What Draya hadn't counted on was somebody suddenly bursting through the kitchen doors and shocking her enough to make her jump. Her arm shifted, and so did the bullet, sending it whizzing past Pea and into the wrong target. Draya's mouth dropped in horror when she saw Jelia's body jerk from the impact of the bullet to her chest. She'd been in the middle of bringing some more dishes to the kitchen and didn't know what she was walking into. The plates in her hands hit the floor and shattered on impact as her hand clutched her chest. Her disbelieving eyes gaped at Draya before she stumbled backward with a look of confusion on her face.

"Oh my God!" Pea screamed, catching her before she hit the ground. "Jelia, Jelia, stay with me!"

Pea applied pressure to the wound, getting blood all over her hands. Draya's breath hitched, and a strangled gasp escaped her lips. It felt as if time had frozen as the reality of what she'd done landed. As she watched Jelia choke on her own blood, trying to get some air, the weight of the gun was suddenly unbearable. She dropped it into her purse and ran out of the kitchen, back into the noisy hallway. The last thing she'd forever remember hearing is Pea's earsplitting, bloodcurdling cry.

"*Rooome!*"

Chapter 22

Rome had been having such a good time partying with his family and friends that he almost forgot that he told Draya to meet him in the parking garage. He wanted to beat her, so he was there waiting for her, but first, he had something for Nami. He found her sitting at a table alone, resting her feet. When she saw him approach the table, she smiled sheepishly.

"My damn feet hurt. Mama told me not to wear these heels with this dress," she said, shaking her head at herself.

"Yeah, well, you know Mama usually knows best," he said and pulled a gift bag from behind his back and handed it to her.

"Is this the part where I act surprised that you got me a gift?" she beamed, taking the bag. "'Cause the truth is, I been waitin' for it all night."

"You just knew I was comin' with somethin' special, huh?" Rome grinned.

"You always do."

"Well, shit, open it."

Nami placed the bag on the table in front of her, took out the tissue paper and peeked inside. She let out a slight squeal when she saw what was on top and did a little dance. Reaching inside, the first thing she pulled out was a thick roll of money.

"You know I love me some money," she said, and quickly stuffed it into her purse, as if someone was going to come and steal it. She reached into the bag again and pulled out two velvet jewelry boxes. She didn't hesitate to open them up, and when she did, she gasped, barely able to speak. "Oh my . . . Ro . . ."

"You a boss now, and no boss can have an empty neck or wrist," he told her.

Nami's face radiated pure delight as she carefully put her new gold Rolex on her wrist. Next, she lifted a golden Cuban link with a gold diamond-encrusted "N" pendant out of its box. It wasn't as big as his, but other than that, it was identical. He took the chain from her and put it around her neck. When he finished, Nami turned around and hugged him tightly.

"Thanks, Ro. I love you."

"I love you more," he said, kissing her on her forehead.

"Damn, Ro, let me hold somethin'," Dru's voice sounded as he approached the table.

"You like?" Nami asked, pulling away from Rome and showing off her new jewelry.

"Hell yeah, got me wantin' to upgrade my own timepiece," Dru said, admiring her watch.

"Speakin' of time . . ." Rome checked his watch, "I'ma be right back."

"Where you going?" Nami asked.

"To the parkin' garage. But can you have Mama or Pea put me up a plate?" he asked.

Nami nodded, and Rome left his siblings at the table. He looked around for Draya but couldn't find her. He hoped he hadn't kept her waiting in the parking garage. It would have ruined the surprise. He dapped up some of his boys on his way out of the party and walked down the hallway that led to the elevator. As he walked, he realized that all of that dancing must have sobered him up some because he barely had a buzz.

He got on the elevator and went down to the lower level, where the parking garage was. Once he stepped off, he pulled a brand-new Mercedes-Benz key fob out of his pocket and clicked a button on it. Immediately, he heard a horn and smiled, knowing he had pulled off the ultimate surprise by having the car delivered during the party. He located where the all-white coupe was and pulled it out so Draya would easily spot it when she got off the elevator. He left the key in the cup holder for her before getting back out and grabbing a big red bow from the backseat to put on the hood of the car. As he was doing that, he heard footsteps and hurried to finish, thinking it was her.

"I bet the last time you saw me, you thought it would be the last time you saw me," a very familiar voice said from behind him.

Suddenly, chills shot down his spine because there was no way possible he should have heard it. Rome stood up straight and slowly turned around, not believing what he was about to see. But that was precisely what he saw. Standing in front of him, impossibly and undeniably, but changed, was Slaw. He was dressed in his usual dapper attire, but the right sleeve of his button-up was rolled up. The skin on his arm was a patchwork of textures, a road map of a fire's cruel kiss. Although healed, the burns left behind a tapestry of discoloration. Rome's blood ran cold as he looked into a set of eyes that burned with intensity. Slaw's face was etched with a grim determination. It was apparent that there was only one thing on his mind: revenge.

"How?" was all Rome could think to ask.

"You'd be surprised about the kind of strength a man can brandish when he has the will to survive," Slaw said. "After you left me there to die, the fire rapidly spread to the kitchen, and as I lay there, inhaling the smoke, I realized I didn't wanna die. Not before I experienced what it was like to be you. The thought of killing you and taking everything you love gave me enough strength to crawl out of that raging inferno. Of course, not before I got a few 'forever memories,' as you can see. I got third-degree burns on my right arm and half of my torso, but I made it out with my life. But barely. While I healed, the only thing I thought about was playing the final piece on my chessboard."

At that second, the sound of the elevator dinging echoed in the garage. Rome looked past Slaw, and, to his horror, he saw Draya round the corner, running toward them. When she got close and saw the scene at hand, she slowed to an uneasy stop. Rome saw her lips trembling and horror in her eyes. Slaw turned to look at her, and knowing he would have no problem hurting her, Rome drew his gun and aimed it at him.

"You shoulda stayed dead," Rome said, and then to Draya, "Baby, close your eyes."

He aimed his weapon at Slaw's head and pulled the trigger without a second thought. However, no bullet came out. The gun just clicked. Rome squeezed it again, but it did the same thing. He stared at it with confusion, and Slaw turned back to face him. An evil laugh came out of his mouth.

"I don't think you have any bullets," Slaw taunted.

"But how?" Rome said more to himself.

"Think about it. Who would have access to your gun, hmm?"

"Nobody except . . ." Rome said, racking his own brain. His gun was only three places. In his car, on his hip or in his bedroom. And nobody had been in his car or his bedroom recently except . . . His eyes widened as he looked at Draya. "You?"

It couldn't be true . . . could it? He loved her. He didn't believe she could do him so dirty. She turned her attention from Rome to Slaw.

"You said he would already be dead before I got down here," she said, confirming Slaw's words were true.

"Your messages were coming slow, so I was a little late to the party," he told her.

"Draya . . .?" Pain dripped from Rome's voice.

"I infiltrated your organization in a few ways, but the best way was with an unhappy woman," Slaw said, chuckling. "All those nights you left her alone led her to me. Not intentionally, of course. Just a fateful night at dinner. When I found out who she was, of course, I was going to use it to my advantage; I just never counted on falling in love with her. You're a fool. You had a diamond, but you were out chasing rocks. Think, Rome. How the fuck do you think I knew about you stashing money at Old Lamont's place? And exactly when you'd be outside the church after the funeral? Who do you think she went to that comedy show with? And who do you think nursed me back to health after you tried to kill me?"

"You bitch!" Rome shouted at Draya as the anger welled up inside of him like a volcano ready to explode. "How could you do this?"

"I told you I wasn't happy," she said with a sad shrug. "I told you I needed more. You didn't listen."

"So you set me up?"

"It . . . It wasn't supposed to be like this."

"You fuckin' my enemy. How did you think it was gon' go? Huh, Draya?"

"After what I've done, we can never go back. I-I'm sorry. I'm so sorry. But this is the life I'm choosing. Slaw loves me in ways that you never did."

"That's enough talking." Slaw waved his hand around in a bored fashion. "By the way, Rome, we appreciate the gifts. The car, oh . . . and the connect. I could have killed you at any time, but I needed that bit of information, and when she got it, well . . . gotta get you outta my way. The city needs a new kingpin."

Rome, furious and feeling completely betrayed, lunged at him, prepared to beat him up as he had before. But Slaw was too quick on the draw. He pulled his gun from his waist and fired one shot into Rome's stomach. Draya jumped at the loud bang and closed her eyes after seeing Rome stop in his tracks. He felt an intense burning sensation from where the bullet entered and grimaced from the pain. He tried to keep his footing as he fell back, but eventually, he collapsed, clutching his stomach.

"Get in the car," Slaw instructed Draya, and she did what she was told, careful not to look at Rome, gravely injured on the concrete floor of the garage. When she was safely in the passenger seat, Slaw came and stood over Rome, glaring down into his eyes. "You remember what I said about them tables turning?"

As he aimed the gun at Rome's forehead with his finger on the trigger, Rome heard the sound of the elevator dinging again in the distance and listened to his name being called by his loved ones. He swore he could feel the vibrations of their feet hitting the pavement as they ran and neared him in the parking garage.

"Rome, Rome! It's Draya. She killed Mama!" he heard Nami screaming.

All the love he ever had in his heart for Draya instantly turned into hatred, and he couldn't do anything about it. Slaw waited until his family rounded the corner, and Rome saw the horror on all their faces, seeing him—the one who couldn't die—helpless and at the mercy of a man who he'd beaten so many times before. Nami screamed, Pea was covered in blood, but she screamed for him too. Jyair and Dru looked at Slaw with the same disbelief as

Rome had when he saw him standing in the garage. Both tried to draw their guns, but they were too late. Slaw's finger happily tugged the trigger, sending a bullet into Rome's head.

"Nooo!" Nami's ear-piercing cry filled the garage as Slaw snatched Rome's signature chain from his neck and ran to the driver's seat of the Mercedes.

Jyair and Dru ran toward them, shooting wildly into the Mercedes. Still, the sound of an engine revving and tires screeching told them that they'd gotten away. Rome felt intense pressure at the front of his head, and he grew weaker by the second, confused and hazy. Blood poured from both wounds, taking his life force with it. Although he hadn't died instantly, he knew he was dying and would be dead at any moment. His eyes were slowly closing as he was losing consciousness, but he fought to hold on for just a few more seconds until his loved ones were by his side. He wanted to see their faces one last time. Nami fell on his body in a sobbing fit, not caring about the blood getting on her pretty birthday dress. Jyair looked helplessly down at him as his eyes scoured around desperately like he was searching for a miracle to help them. Rome heard Pea begging him to stay with them. He wanted to tell her he didn't want to leave, but the words never found his mouth. Dru, smoking gun in his hand, dropped to his knees beside him. His head hung low as a heavy sob escaped his mouth. The last thing Rome felt before letting go of his final breath, and everything went dark, was his little brother's tears falling on his cheek.

Part Two

Twenty-five Years Later . . .

Chapter 23

The delicious smell of bacon sizzling snuck its way under the closed bedroom door of a spacious master bedroom. It was enough to make the young man sleeping in the king-sized bed stir slightly. However, he was sure that he was dreaming. There wasn't anyone in his home but him, or there wasn't supposed to be anyway. It wasn't until he heard the music playing that he knew he wasn't alone, but when he opened his eyes, he didn't panic. Instead, he stretched big and looked over at the clock on the nightstand beside his bed. It read five minutes after ten in the morning. He groaned because that meant he'd overslept. The night before had been a long one, but in his world of work, that was to be expected. He rubbed the sleep out of his eyes and forced himself to wake up completely so he wouldn't fall back asleep again. Then someone knocked at his door. Before he could say, "Come in," it flung open.

"Good, you're up, baby," a sweet voice said as a woman entered with a smile on her face.

She was light skinned, and, although in her early fifties, she still had a youthful appearance and a nice, fit body. Her hair was cut short in a pixie style, and her curls were juicy that morning. She stood there, wearing a pale pink Lululemon legging set and holding a plate full of food so fresh that steam still rose from it.

"Mama, just because you have a key doesn't mean you can just come in my crib whenever you feel like it," he said, sitting up.

"Why doesn't it?"

"Because the lease says 'Toosie Wells,' not 'Draya Wells,'" he said, but still didn't hesitate to take the food from her.

One thing Draya didn't have or know was boundaries when it came to her son, and that was the main reason Toosie had moved away from home in the first place. If Draya had it her way, Toosie would have stayed home in the family mansion for the rest of his life. But Toosie was his own man, and he wanted to prove to his father that even though he worked for him, he could stand on his own two feet. Toosie scarfed down the French toast, grits, eggs and bacon, not caring that everything was still hot. He liked eating his food fresh to wake up his senses. His mother sat at the edge of the bed, watching him in a dreamlike trance.

"You eat just like your father," she noted with a smile.

"Dad would never finish his plate this fast," Toosie reminded her with a grin and handed her his cleared plate.

His father, Slaw Wells, was a very particular man who didn't rush anything, including eating. He liked to take his time, especially when it came to business. He liked to keep his mind clear to make sound decisions at all times, a trait he tried to pass down to his sons, but Toosie was the type to move fast. In his mind, if he made the right decisions, it didn't matter how quickly he did it. And even if it was the wrong choice, he could fix it just as fast.

"You're right," Draya said and patted the part of the comforter where his knee was. "But it's time for you to get up. Your brother is in the kitchen waiting for you."

"Cairo's here too?" Toosie asked. "Do y'all know anything about callin' first?"

"We did. Your ass was asleep." She raised her brows at him. "What did you two get into last night that got you so tired?"

"Nothin' I wanna worry you with," Toosie replied and felt a heaviness overcome him as the events from the night before came back to him.

"Does it have anything to do with those bloody clothes right there?" she asked, pointing at the small pile of clothes in the far corner of the bedroom.

From where he sat in his bed, with the light from the sun, he could clearly see the blood splatters on the jeans. They didn't belong to him or his brother. He looked away, knowing the lecture was coming.

"You know better than to shit where you lie. Whatever the fuck y'all did, those clothes shoulda never made it into this house. Get rid of them immediately and treat this room, do you understand?"

"Mama, I ain't no kid. I know."

"I can't tell. And does that blood have anything to do with Luther William's son getting killed last night in the West End?" she asked, and when Toosie looked surprised, she gave him a knowing look. "Your father has been up all morning trying to clean up this shit after Cairo called and told him what happened. Y'all were supposed to look after that boy. Now, he's dead. What happened?"

Toosie looked away from her. Although he was 25, she had a way of making him feel like a child, especially when she locked her eyes on him like that. It was almost impossible not to tell her the truth. He sighed heavily and shrugged his shoulders.

"We went out to a few clubs last night. The last one we went to Cairo got into it with some boys in the parking lot. I was tryin'a calm him down, but you know his temper. Lex wasn't makin' shit no better. He was hypin' the shit up and pulled his gun out first. Before I knew it, bullets was flyin', and Lex was on the ground dead."

A flash of Lex getting struck in the head by a bullet and dropping to the ground played in his head. Toosie knew the second he saw all the blood spilling out that Lex was dead. He still tried to get him out of the club, but Cairo snatched Toosie away so they could get out of there before the police came.

"Shit," Draya groaned. "This ain't good. What the hell were y'all doing over there to begin with? You know your father doesn't want you anywhere near that part of the city—period. Who did Cairo get into it with?"

"Some dudes. Twins. We gon' handle it, Mama," Toosie answered, and a worried line formed on her forehead.

"You better. Your father wants you both to meet him at his office downtown. This is going to affect his business. As I said, Cairo is here already, so hurry up and get dressed. And don't keep my husband waiting. Set those clothes by the door. I'll take care of them."

Toosie took note of the troubled look on her face as she left the room with his empty plate in her hands. But Toosie didn't give it much more thought because he knew her last statement wasn't a request. It was an order.

The first thing he did when he got up was bag up his bloody clothes to dispose of when he left. Next, he went into his closet and grabbed some clean clothes to wear for the day. Toosie had an eye for fashion, so whether on a good day or a bad day, he was going to look like something. He chose a pair of Amiri jeans and an off-white shirt with the matching shoes before taking a quick shower, although he'd taken one the night before. And just like the night before, he was able to get his body clean, but his thoughts weren't so easily washed away.

Lex had been six foot and 200 pounds of all muscle. Seeing him drop so easily was a sight Toosie couldn't seem to get out of his head. True enough, it wasn't the first time he'd seen a dead body. In fact, he had a few souls under his own belt. However, he just knew that specific death was going to come with some major consequences. Lex's father, Luther, was the owner of Williams Enterprise, a multinational weapons and technology conglomerate. His company supplied many companies and even some government agencies with weapons, both legally and illegally, if the price was right. Lex had been in town in his father's stead, wrapping up a business deal with Slaw. Cairo and Toosie had been charged with showing him a good time on his last night in the city.

When he was fully dressed, he placed his diamond chain around his neck and checked his fly in his bedroom mirror. His hair was freshly braided in long, individual braids that hung loosely around his face. He rubbed his thin mustache and short goatee while studying his smooth, caramel-colored face, looking for any signs of distress. There was a little in his light brown eyes, but that was only because he didn't know what his father was going to do.

He grabbed the bag of clothes before leaving the bedroom of his condo, then walked down the hallway and went to the kitchen, where his big brother, Cairo, was sitting there, waiting for him. Cairo was the spitting image of Slaw when he was his age, right down to the way he dressed. That day, he was wearing a pair of fitted pants and a button-up. He had deep waves in his hair, which he'd recently gotten cut and shaped up, and was calmly finishing his breakfast when Toosie entered.

"'Bout time you got up. Pop wants us to come see him," he said, wiping his hands off on a napkin.

"I know. My mama told me," Toosie said and looked around. "She left?"

"Yeah." Cairo nodded to the bag in Toosie's hand. "She said to leave that by the front door. She'll come get it later and have somebody clean ya crib. You burnt out for not burnin' them before steppin' foot in here."

"I know. But what's burnt out is you not bein' able to control ya temper—as always," Toosie shot back.

"Aye, didn't nobody tell that motherfucka to pull out his fire. He got his own self killed."

"Is that what you gon' tell Dad?"

"Shit, we got to tell him somethin'," Cairo shrugged.

"I still can't believe it happened. Shit just happened so fast."

"It don't matter; it happened. Cry at the funeral. The only thing we need to concern ourselves with is the fact that he got killed while he was with us. We gotta smooth it out so the money don't get fucked up."

Cairo stood up from the table and took his empty plate to the sink. Toosie took notice of his callousness and how he didn't even seem affected by Lex's death. The only thing on his mind was getting back to the money. Toosie wondered whether he felt guilty and was trying to hide it, or whether he truly felt nothing at all.

"I be tellin' you all the time ya temper gon' get us fucked up one day. Now look. The fuck them boys even say to you to set you off?" Toosie asked.

"They ain't have to say shit. They was just disrespectful. Bumped into me and looked at me like I was trash and started talkin' shit."

"Words is words."

"Not when they comin' from the other side," Cairo said. "I don't know why Pop don't just let us kill all of 'em."

"How you know?" Toosie asked and made a face.

"You seen how them boys was dressed. And them was real diamonds on they necks. They gettin' to some real pape."

"Not like us, though. Dad is the biggest boss in the city. He not worried about a little corner piece. Now, let's go face the music 'cause you let some words bruise ya ego."

Before they left, Toosie dropped the bag in his hand by the front door for his mom when she returned. He knew she would make good on her word and get rid of the clothing, and he looked forward to having a spotless place when he came home.

Chapter 24

The sound of humming filled the big kitchen of a beautiful, two-story, Victorian-style home. A beautiful woman in her sixties bustled around making breakfast under the brightness of the low-hanging light fixtures. The kitchen was her happy place and had been designed and tailored to her liking. She wore a pink apron over her cream-colored jogging suit that said, "*Stay Out Of My Way While I'm Cooking,*" and by the concentrated look on her face, she meant it. She was in the middle of flipping pancakes, making them perfectly with crisp edges, just like her family liked. There was a flat-screen television on the wall, and the morning news was playing.

"Late last night at a popular nightclub, The Plaza, a fatal shooting occurred. One person is reported dead. No suspects are in custody at the moment."

After hearing that, she grabbed the remote on the counter beside her and flipped the channel.

"Nope, not subscribing to that mess this morning. Not at all," she mumbled to herself before putting down the remote and going to get the bacon out of the oven.

She finished cooking and took the food into the dining room. She had made a delicious-looking spread full of everyone's favorites, which wasn't unusual, since she loved to cook, especially in her later years. In the distance, she heard multiple footsteps bounding down the stairs and smirked to herself, knowing that the aroma from the kitchen had traveled throughout the house. She went back into the kitchen and, sure enough, was met by the identical faces of her handsome twin grandsons, Jah and Zilla. They were completely identical at their factory settings. Both had a light complexion, chiseled faces and full lips. Their eyes were light brown, a trait they'd gotten from their mother's side of the family, and both were well over six feet like their father. But after that, the two couldn't have been more different. Zilla kept his thick hair cut short and had waves so deep, the ocean would be jealous. He also had tattoos covering his arms, chest and neck. Jah, on the other hand, had soft, shoulder-length locs and no tattoos at all. They were early birds, fully dressed in their usual slim-fitting jeans, designer shirts and shoes. Zilla stood there with a large stack of money in his hands, eagerly looking around the kitchen.

"Nana Pea, I smell the food, but I don't see the food," he said, hugging her and kissing her on the cheek.

"It's already on the table, baby," she said, reaching up, pinching his cheek. "But what have I said about you bringing your work into the dining room?"

"My bad, Nana, I was in the middle of countin' when I smelled pancakes."

"Nana, this boy ran out of his room like he never had pancakes before," Jah said, laughing, and also gave her a good morning hug.

"Shit, that's what he's supposed to do when he knows I done busted my butt in this kitchen for y'all."

"Plus, I'm hungry after last night. We didn't even get no food after—" Zilla tried to say, but Jah nudged him to stop him midsentence.

"After what?" Nana Pea asked, raising her brow.

"Nothin'," Zilla said and disappeared into the dining room.

"Mm-hmm," she said, not believing him. "Where's your mother?"

"Upstairs in her room," Jah told her. "She probably won't come down, but I'll take her a plate."

"You're a good boy. Now, wash your hands and tell that brother of yours to do the same . . . having that dirty-ass money at my dinner table. Ain't no telling where it's been."

The words were barely out of her mouth when she heard the loud slamming of the front door coming from the foyer. Since the house was large, she would only be able to hear it from the kitchen if it was done forcefully.

"Y'all was shootin' in public? Are y'all stupid, or are y'all just fuckin' stupid?" the loud voice boomed before anyone appeared in the kitchen.

Jah froze and looked at Nana Pea when two men entered the kitchen. One of them was his father, Jyair, and the other his uncle Dru. Jyair looked to be so angry that he couldn't speak, but Dru had no issue belting out his words. He'd come in with fiery eyes and clenched fists. The anger was evident on his face, and even Pea knew not to move. Not because she was scared, but because she had known Dru since he was younger, and he didn't play. She wanted to protect her grandson just in case his uncle pounced.

"Where the hell is ya brother?" Dru asked, looking around.

"Zilla, get in here," Nana Pea called, knowing that Zilla was probably in there stuffing his face with no worry in the world.

He came slinking into the kitchen, and his eyes went from Jah to his father and then finally to his uncle. Although both Dru and Jyair were pushing 50, they had aged gracefully into what women of those days called "zaddy" status. Both were still dressed stylishly and rocked their long hair in various styles just as they had when they were younger. Although they had gray on their heads and faces, neither had a wrinkle, most likely due to the vitamins Dru's sister and Jyair's wife, Nami, made them take daily. Jyair hadn't said a word. Instead, he looked at his sons with a stoic look that could even quiet a ravenous bear.

"So . . . I guess y'all heard about what happened last night," Zilla said, looking like he was happy for the island separating them all.

"Heard about it? It's all over the news. Triston's daughter is the one who told him it was y'all doin' the shootin'!"

"Triston ain't taught Tesa to keep her mouth shut?" Jah asked, making a face.

"She ain't talkin' to the police; she's talkin' to her father who works for me," Dru said, glaring at him. "How the fuck you think it feels for someone to tell me that my nephews are out here bein' stupid and reckless?"

"I mean, some people stepped to us, so we stepped back," Zilla said with a shrug. "What's the big deal? You told me you and Uncle Ro got into a lot of fights back in the day over your respect."

"That shit was different. And this wasn't no fight. Y'all had a whole fuckin' shoot-out."

"They upped the pole first, Unc. What was we s'posed to do? Sit around and get shot?"

"Lay down and beg 'em not to hurt us like some hoes?" Jah threw in, and Zilla found himself smirking, which made Dru even madder.

"Y'all so fuckin' stupid. Do y'all even *know* who you killed? Lexington Williams!"

"I don't care 'bout no names. Far as I know, they was just some hatin'-ass clowns in the club. Dropped 'em and kept it pushin'."

"Zilla, did you just hear what I said?" Dru looked like he wanted to kill him.

Instead, he clenched and unclenched his fists before taking a seat at one of the island stools. He briefly put his head in his hands as he tried to calm himself. Finally, he looked up at Jyair, who still hadn't said a word.

"Jy, ya sons are idiots. They don't know what they've just done."

Jyair crossed his arms over his chest and allowed his gaze to shift between the two boys, his eyes lingering on each face. A heavy silence fell over the kitchen, but just because no actual words were exchanged didn't mean communication wasn't happening. The disappointment dripped from Jyair's whole body language, and it was that which made the twins shrink and realize they'd done something bad.

"Dad, I—" Jah tried to say, but Jyair held up a hand, quieting him.

"Pop, we—" Zilla tried, but he too was silenced.

"Ask the right question or shut the fuck up," Jyair finally said icily.

The twins looked at each other and seemed to speak silently. They both agreed that they'd messed up. The tone of voice their father used was one only reserved for them when he was extremely pissed off. It was usually their mother who chastised them if they made a mistake; Jyair usually guided them through it. But right then, he was fed up. Zilla took a breath and tried again.

"What did we do?" he asked.

"You killed the son of a wealthy and powerful man with a lot of powerful connections," Jyair told them. "And he ain't gon' just let that shit go. Not to mention a police investigation."

"We got the security footage already from the club. Cost us ten bands, but we made sure there wasn't a backup drive," Jah reassured his dad.

"But what about eyewitnesses?" Dru asked.

"He upped his gun on us first, Unc. Even if somebody talk, we had a right to defend ourselves. Plus, ain't no murder weapon. We don't know fa sho who hit 'em, so we got rid of both the fires," Jah explained.

"Either way, one thing we know is it's gon' get back to Luther that it was one of you two who killed his son. It's no secret that he's Slaw's weapons dealer." Suddenly, Dru made a thoughtful face. "Who was Lex with last night?"

"Two other dudes. They was shootin' at us too. One of 'em had light brown eyes."

"Like yours?" Nana Pea asked.

"Yeah, kinda, why?"

Nana Pea didn't say anything; instead, she, Dru and Jyair exchanged a look. Suddenly, all the lightheartedness and happiness she had felt that morning evaporated. It was replaced with a sense of regret and longing.

"I need the two of you to lie low for a while until me and Jy figure this shit out. I have no doubt in my mind that they're tryin'a figure out who y'all are. And if Luther and Slaw are as close as I think they are, he gon' have some powerful forces behind him to get his get back."

"I ain't scared of no fuckin' Slaw. That's *y'all.*" Zilla's outburst was an angry one. He hit the island in front of him with his fist.

"Aye, bruh, chill," Jah tried to calm him. But Zilla ignored him.

"I would love to go at that motherfucka. Somebody needs to. He the reason Mama hates her own birthday. She done barely came out of her room in a week, and her birthday is in two days. I'm not scared of no beef."

"Li'l boy, you think it's the beef we scared of?" Dru asked, turning his nose up at him. "I done went heads up with Slaw more times than I can count, and I can tell you fa sho, that man is a bitch. I watched my brother whoop him with his bare hands. We scared of losin' you two dumbasses 'cause you new age motherfuckas think with ya trigger instead of ya head. We need a game plan so even if they do send whoever, they know we still not to be fucked with."

"I'm not a little boy," Zilla murmured under his breath, but he didn't get loud again.

"Yeah, Pop, Unc. We not little boys. Fuck just defendin' ourselves. Y'all don't think it's time we flip the tables back to when Uncle Rome was runnin' things? I'm tired of the scraps. I wanna see some major paper. Maybe this is the perfect reason to kill him and take back what's rightfully ours."

"Flippin' them tables ain't somethin' that's gon' come easy, son," Jyair told him with a sigh. "When Ro was runnin' things, we had a lot more manpower and a lot more people loyal to us. After he got killed, a literal shift occurred in the city and much of that loyalty died with him, including the empire he built. People went to where the money was at. Our old boys in the main circle? The ones supposed to be the most solid? Leon, Abram and Triston's twin brother, Jax? They turned on us the moment they thought the well was gon' dry."

"Stupid motherfuckas," Dru scoffed. "They really thought Slaw was gon' let 'em live? Bodies turned up all over the city. That's why Triston helps me run the car washes, but he ain't fuckin' with the game ever again. They sent different parts of Jax's body for weeks and saved the head for last. That shit fucked him up."

"Damn," Jah said, shaking his head.

"Damn is right. And that's why I need you boys to lie low for a while. If y'all need to go anywhere, take ya cousin Mike Mike with you," Jyair said. "I don't need shit else happenin' before ya mama's surprise birthday party Sunday. Understand?"

"Understood," Zilla and Jah said in unison.

"Now, get in there and eat. Don't forget to make your mama's plate," Nana Pea instructed them. Before Zilla could walk away, though, she snatched him up by his shirt. "Go wash them hands, boy."

"Yes, ma'am," he said, laughing.

She smiled and let him go. When both boys were out of the kitchen, the smile on her face waned, and she turned her attention to Dru and Jyair. They had both grown to be like the sons she never had, just like Rome had been. Dru and Nami had lost both their brother and their mother on the same day. It was a rocky time there for a minute, and Nana Pea had to step up to the plate. She couldn't take the place of their mother, but she knew they needed her, and she couldn't leave. She was there when Jyair and Nami got married. She was also there for the birth of their sons, where both parents asked her to be their grandmother. It was the same thing when Dru had his daughter, Dior. They were her family now, the same one that Rome had promised her all those years ago. And she would protect them until she had no more life in her.

Even though Dru hadn't been ready to take on the role as head of the family, he did it. He, Jyair and their close friend, Melo, formed their own small operation using Rome's connects, which he'd gotten from his uncle Charlie. Although Slaw was able to backdoor them and take Rome's major plug from him, Rome had just gotten an order in right before he died. That was what Dru used to start them off. Of course, Slaw tried over the years to get rid of them, but Dru was Rome's little brother and built to last. After a while, Slaw just stopped, and things had been quiet ever since.

"Do you think . . ." Nana Pea finally said, but her voice trailed off.

"That my sons almost killed their cousin? Yeah," Jyair said, sighing. "This shit is fucked up."

"We need to tell them," Nana Pea said, and looked at Dru. "All of them, including Dior."

"Nah," Dru said, shaking his head, thinking about the son his brother never even knew he was going to have. "It ain't the time, and it might never be. He might have Ro's blood in his veins, but that's Slaw's boy."

Chapter 25

Standing silhouetted against the floor-to-ceiling window was Slaw, a solitary figure in his expansive office above downtown Atlanta. The city sprawled beneath him as the movement stretched beyond where his eyes could see. The air in his office was thick with the rich aroma of the Cuban cigar between his fingers, its smoke curling lazily around his head like a crown. His eyes narrowed slightly, fixed on the scene below. He took in the frenetic energy and began to get lost in the distant hum of traffic and the faint wail of sirens.

Usually, his mornings were filled with reflection on how he'd come so far and built such a grand empire. He'd turned dirty money into a never-ending fountain and was the most untouchable man in the whole city. However, that morning was different . . . because the boys who he'd raised to be men had ruined it.

Slaw had his hands in many things, but the most lucrative was becoming a silent partner in Luther Williams's weapons business, Williams Enterprise. The truth was, Luther wouldn't have been able to start the company up without Slaw's money, and what the world didn't know was that Slaw held the biggest share of the company. Still, that would make it no easier on him that Luther's youngest son had been killed while out with Slaw's.

With money as long as Slaw's, he could make anything go away. Anyone who had seen anything at The Plaza the night before had been paid off before the morning sun had even risen. And if anyone thought to speak up or slipped through the cracks, he had many officers and detectives on his payroll who would have no issue getting rid of the problem for him. But once again, that served no good for Luther, who no longer had his child.

Slaw stepped away from the window and walked over to a painting that hung on his wall. On his way to it, he placed his cigar in an ashtray on his desk. The painting was a mural of a man slaying another in combat. Both were in armor, but one lay on the ground bleeding out while the other stood over him, victorious, holding a bloody sword. However, as one's eyes began to travel around the painting, they'd see many dead men lying around in various positions, slain by the victor's sword. The scene was brutal, and the smile on the victor's face showed the true beast inside of man. The painting reminded him of himself. He placed a hand on the side of it and pulled it open like a door. Behind it was a safe where he punched in a code and opened it.

Inside was a pistol, a few stacks of money, and some poker chips, but his eyes moved past them. They fell on one of his most outstanding tokens. At the back of the safe, lying effortlessly on a jewelry stand, was a golden Cuban link chain with a huge diamond-encrusted pendant. He stared at the big C for a moment. A slow smile crept to his face as he remembered the day he'd come into power. The day he'd killed the great Rome and stolen the crown and the city. He wanted to relish in the feeling for much longer, but a knock at his office door interrupted the moment. Closing the safe and returning the painting to its spot, he turned around and went over to his large office desk.

"Come in," he said loudly once he was settled in his seat.

The door opened, and in walked exactly who he had been waiting for, his sons. Cairo, his firstborn, walked in cockily and like no one on earth could touch him. Even though he knew the reason for the meeting, his tail wasn't tucked, and his head was deliberately high, purposely walking in front of his brother. Toosie, on the other hand, had a subtle confidence about him. As if he knew he didn't have to do too much to be seen or noticed. He didn't care to be the first or the last, because when he arrived . . . he arrived.

"You look good, Pop." Cairo complimented his father's fashionable attire when they were directly in front of him.

"Flattery will get you nowhere," Slaw said evenly and motioned to the chairs on the other side of the desk. "Sit down, both of you."

When they did, the polished mahogany of the desk seemed to reflect the gravity of the moment. Although they were men of considerable stature, they were just boys with vulnerability that only Slaw could elicit under his powerful gaze. Both of their eyes, usually sharp and confident, were downcast, trying to avoid their father's. Slaw's presence alone was a force in itself as he sat ramrod straight with disappointment radiating from his body. The silence in the room was thick. Cairo, usually one with the gift of gab, said nothing.

"You both know you fucked up, right?" Slaw asked. "What were you thinking? The boy was only here for a few days. You couldn't keep him alive that long?"

"It's not our fault," Cairo said, and Slaw took note of the side eye Toosie gave him. "Everything just happened too fast."

"What's 'everything'?" Slaw asked, and Cairo grew silent again, so Slaw posed his question to Toosie. "Tyri Jr. . . . what's 'everything'?"

Toosie looked uncomfortable, and Slaw could tell that he knew something. However, his loyalty to his brother was preventing him from saying it. He had already figured that whatever happened had stemmed from Cairo. He loved his son, and he was the oldest of the two boys, but he lacked leadership qualities. Since his youth, he has shown an inability to make sound decisions. He was smart, yes. And ruthless as ever, but he was a hothead who let his emotions get the best of him.

"I got into it with these two dudes. Twins. They disrespected me," Cairo reluctantly said when Toosie didn't speak.

"How?" Slaw asked.

"One of 'em bumped into me. I felt like he did it on purpose, and then they both looked at me like I was trash. Like I was a bitch or somethin'. So I showed 'em I wasn't. I ain't pull my gun out first, though. That was Lex," Cairo said.

"Replay the whole situation in your head. Was it worth it?" Slaw asked him, and Cairo clenched his jaw. Slaw barked louder. "*Was* it? Somebody bumping into you got my business partner's son killed—in the middle of the biggest deal of the year?"

"No."

"No," Slaw repeated and allowed a condescending laugh to escape his lips. "Which is why I think you're the biggest fool there ever was. Luther Williams will be here this afternoon and will want to know why his son is dead. You mean me to tell him the reason why is because somebody *bumped* you?"

The way Slaw glared at Cairo, one might not have even thought he was his son. He didn't know whether to be disappointed or angry. Both seemed fitting. Cairo couldn't help but fidget uncomfortably, and seeing that, Toosie came to his rescue.

"Dad, Lex is dead because of Lex. Not 'cause of us," Toosie spoke up. "Yeah, there was an argument, and Cairo lost his temper as he does sometimes, but it was just words. It didn't get to a deadly point until Lex pulled out his gun. I don't think we put *him* in danger. He did that to himself."

"You're missing the point," Slaw said, shaking his head. "You shouldn't have even been on that side of town in the first place. I grew up over there, and it's a cutthroat place. Kill or be killed. You boys came up in the drug game with an already-made kingdom. Born millionaires. Over there, they're creating shit from shit, piss and mud. That means they have a different kind of hunger and respect for the game."

"You saying we're not hungry?"

"I'm saying you fucked up. And this time, I'm going to make you responsible for cleaning up your own mess. I need you to find and bring me the ones who killed Lex expeditiously. I can imagine Luther wanting to kill them himself." The boys nodded, but before they left his office, Slaw held up a hand to stop them. "And, Cairo?"

"Yeah, Pop?"

"From now on, your roles will be reversed. Toosie will be responsible for meeting with the supplier and distro. You can make the money rounds."

"*What?*" Cairo made a face at hearing he'd been stripped of his rank in the business.

Beside him, Toosie looked at their father, shocked. He had never done distro. Ever since Slaw had gotten too busy running his many businesses, he had put Cairo in charge of meeting with the supplier every month to get their product.

"I can't trust you. I can't have someone with such temperamental problems in charge of something so important."

"When have I ever fucked up the money?"

"Last night. Not only that, but also your inability to walk away put you and your brother in harm's way. Your mother and I—"

"That woman . . . *isn't* my mother," Cairo interrupted icily.

"Draya helped raise you since you were 2 when your mother ran out on you because I didn't want to be with her. She's as much your mother as I am your father, and you will never disrespect her in my presence. Your ego is a problem, and it needs to be reminded that you are a part of someone else's program—mine. Toosie understands that and doesn't let his pride get in the way of the bigger picture, my fucking money. You'll follow his lead from now on."

"I'm not about to be ordered around by my little brother."

"You can, and you will. If I even get wind of you not following a direct order, you won't have any place in my business at all, and when I'm gone, *everything* will go to Toosie. Then you'll *have* to listen to him, won't you?"

"Dad, you don't gotta do this. We made a mistake, and we'll fix it, but you don't gotta demote Cairo. We can keep our usual positions."

"Just like he doesn't have a choice, you don't either. You'll meet with Rafael and handle the next order. Is that understood?" Slaw said, and Toosie nodded. "Now, both of you, get out of my office and find the motherfuckas who killed Luther's boy."

Once dismissed, Cairo forcefully pushed his chair back as he got up and stormed out of the office. Toosie looked like he was caught in the middle of a tight place. He looked at his father and nodded, seemingly accepting his new role, and calmly got up and left the office. Slaw knew he'd made the best decision for the moment. The only one who could prove him wrong was Toosie.

Chapter 26

A knock at her bedroom door did the one thing that the light filtering through Nami's bedroom window couldn't: wake her up. She put her covers over her head and tried to ignore the loud knocking. She'd already sent her son Zilla away when he tried to bring her breakfast. She hadn't had an appetite for days. All she wanted to do that morning was sleep in. Finally, the knocking stopped, and she thought that whoever was in the hallway outside of her bedroom had gotten the hint. But, of course, that was too good to be true. The next knock was loud and deliberate.

"Auntie Nami, it's me, Dior. Can I come in?" she heard the sweet voice of her niece.

Nami threw her covers down and sighed as she looked up at the master bedroom's vast ceiling. Obviously, nobody was going to allow her to get her rest. She couldn't catch a break.

"Yes. Come in," she called.

The door flew open, and in walked her gorgeous 21-year-old niece. Nami always told Dru that genes were a crazy thing because she looked exactly like her brother, just in a female body. Ever since Dior was a little girl, she'd attached herself to Nami's hip and had become her shadow. So much so that she'd followed in her footsteps and gone into the beauty industry too. However, instead of being a hairdresser, she became an esthetician, which allowed her to work in her aunt's massive studio.

"You look pretty," Nami said, instantly softening at the sight of her.

If she hadn't gone into the beauty industry, Dior would have found a home in fashion. The girl could dress her butt off with her eyes closed, and she loved treating herself like a Barbie. That morning, she wore a fitted graphic baby tee, an army fatigue skirt with a flare and platform boots. An oversized Louis Vuitton bag hung on her arm, and her hair was freshly done in a just-past-the-shoulder-length blunt cut bob with a middle part. She usually loved playing with hair colors, but that time she'd opted for plain black. As an esthetician, she said she was her own promotion, so, of course, her skin was smooth, and her lash extensions were always on point.

"And you look crazy," Dior said, widening her eyes at Nami's bed head. "Since when don't you sleep with your bonnet on?"

She made a face as she picked up a piece of Nami's hair, looking at it as if she'd never seen anything like it. Nami swatted her hand away and sat up, getting a glance at herself in the full-length corner mirror in the bedroom. She had to admit she did look a little crazy. She was wearing one of her husband's shirts, which was extremely oversized on her, and her hair truly was an all-over-the-place mess.

"I couldn't find it last night," she said and tried to smooth down her hair.

"That ain't gon' do nothin'. You need a comb and a brush—hell, a flat iron too. Come on, I'll do it," Dior said and tried to pull her aunt out of bed.

"Aht aht!" Nami said, pulling away from her. "I'm not going anywhere. Why do I need to do my hair?"

"Because we *are* going somewhere, and you can't come with me lookin' like you lost a fight with a werewolf. Heck . . . You look *like* the werewolf."

"Girl, don't make me hurt you," Nami warned, pointing her finger at Dior.

"Seriously, Auntie, you are too fine to be up in here like this. Ever since I was little, I was so proud to have a baddie for an aunt, *and* you don't look your age. Come on, you can't go out sad like this."

Dior was right. At almost 45, Nami could still give a woman half her age the blues. However, recently, she'd been giving herself the blues, not wanting to get up, go out or do anything, for that matter. And she knew why. Her birthday was around the corner, and it just wasn't a celebration anymore. It was a reminder of the day she lost two of the people she loved the most in the world. She just never could find any joy on that day since she turned 20. Her whole life changed in a matter of minutes. On a day-to-day basis, she seemed fine and able to function, but every year when her birthday neared, she couldn't help the depressed state she got in. She couldn't fend off the flood of memories she had with her mother and Rome. Many of them brought her great joy, but the highs came with the lowest low of remembering them lying on the ground in pools of their own blood.

That had been the worst day of her life, and after that, many more bad days followed. She hadn't just lost a mother that day; she lost her guidance. She hadn't just lost a brother; she lost her friend and her protector. She'd do anything to hug him or dance with him again as they'd done for so long that fateful night. Nami hadn't been able to celebrate her birthday since. She would rather be left alone or catch up on her rest . . . like she was trying to do right then.

"I'm not going out sad. In fact, I'm not going out anywhere," Nami grumbled, lying back down and throwing the cover back over her head.

"Auntie, come on. We have to go find you a dress to umm . . . make you feel better."

Dior gripped the cover and yanked it back down just as Nami was rolling her eyes. Her husband thought that he was being slick by planning her a surprise birthday party, but he seemed to have forgotten that he'd married one of the nosiest people on the planet. Weeks ago, Nami had seen the reservation for a party hall along with deposits paid to a caterer and decorator. She wasn't stupid. Even though it was just him trying to do something sweet for his wife, it was going to hurt his feelings when she wasn't in attendance.

"I'm not going to the party," she said dryly and turned her head just in time to see Dior's eyes widen.

"You know about the party?"

"My husband has always been terrible at keeping secrets from me. He told me in many ways without actually saying it."

"Then you know how hard he's worked to put all this together for you."

"This is for him and y'all. He knows I don't care to celebrate my birthday. Not after . . ." her voice trailed off, and her eyes got distant.

Seeing this, Dior sighed and sat down on the side of the bed. She let her body fall onto her auntie and gave her the biggest hug. Nami's arms squeezed her as she hugged her back. When she pulled away, Nami had a few tears in her eyes that she quickly flicked away.

"I know I never got to meet him, but I know Uncle Ro was that guy back in the day. You don't talk about him, but Daddy does, and he says he used to take care of y'all like his own kids even though you were so close in age," Dior said softly, and Nami nodded in confirmation. "Daddy told me about the night he died, which was really hard for him to talk about. But one thing he always says is that it was the best and worst night of his life. The worst because he lost his mom and brother. But the best was that he had never seen you smile so big. He said you, him and Uncle Ro danced and danced. He also said Uncle Ro was sneakin' you jungle juice all night."

"He did," a laugh found its way out of Nami's mouth. "It was so good too."

"From what I've heard about him, I don't think he would want you lying in this bed instead of shoppin' for your birthday. And, plus . . ." she reached into her purse and pulled out a large stack of money. "Today, everything is on me."

"Girl, I have a husband," Nami said, seeing the plea written all over Dior's perfectly symmetrical face. "Everything is going to be on him. Put your money away, girl."

Dior squealed in delight and jumped up from the bed. She dropped the money into her purse and waited for Nami to get out of bed. Only then did she go to the bedroom door and step out.

"You got half an hour, ma'am."

Dior left Nami to get up and get ready. Nami still didn't have any plans for going to any party, but the more she thought about it, a shopping day didn't sound too bad. She pushed open the door to her en suite bathroom and flicked on the lights, feeling the cool inside welcome her immediately. Her bare feet became one with the heated tile floor as she walked to the shower and stripped free of her clothing. The stone slabs of the shower walls gleamed in the ambient light, the marble's subtle veining catching her eye. She reached out and turned on the shower, adjusting the temperature until it was just right. Steam began to fill the glass enclosure, swirling around the stone bench inside. Nami slid the glass door fully open and stepped in, then closed it behind her.

The first droplets of water hit her skin, and a rush of heat made her shiver involuntarily. As she moved fully in the range of the showerhead, the water cascaded over her, loosening the tension in her shoulders and back. It felt like a warm embrace, melting away the stress that had been trying to consume her. She closed her eyes and tilted her face up to the water, letting it wash over her. Next, she reached for her washcloth and her favorite soap, knowing that she could get lost in that shower forever. And knowing Dior, she would really be back in thirty minutes to check on her. She cleaned herself and rinsed off a few times before getting out and wrapping a towel around her body. While the steam in the bathroom settled, she moisturized herself, then walked into the connecting closet to find something to wear. It didn't take long for her to decide on a long, peach-colored spaghetti-strapped dress and a pair of sandals.

Once she pulled her hair back into a tight bun and she was dressed, Nami grabbed a Chanel bag and left her room. She almost ran right into Dior, who was marching down the hallway with conviction. She probably thought her aunt had gotten back into bed, but was outwardly pleased to see Nami looking like herself. Dior linked their arms together and guided Nami down the hallway and down the stairs like she didn't know how to get around her own house. Standing in the foyer, seemingly waiting for them, were both of her sons.

"Y'all ready?" Zilla asked just as Nana Pea rounded the corner, holding a basket of laundry.

"Where do you and your brother think y'all are going?" she asked, giving him and Zilla a confused look. "Didn't your dad say that he wanted you in the house?"

"Nah, he said he wanted us to lie low. Not that we couldn't go with Ma to Lenox," Jah told her with a grin.

"Your mom?" Nana Pea turned her head, and it was then that Pea noticed Nami and Dior on the stairs. Her eyes beamed. "Finally, you leave your evil lair."

"Dior wants to take me shopping," Nami said, but looked curiously at her sons. "Why does your father want you to lie low?"

"Just business stuff," Jah said quickly. "Nothin' too crazy. He ain't gon' trip on us escortin' our mother shoppin'. Huh, Nana?"

"Uh-uh. I ain't in it," Nana Pea rolled her eyes and started up the stairs. As she passed Nami, she kissed her on the cheek. "Have a good time, honey. I'll have somethin' for you to eat when you get home."

As she passed, Nami gave her sons a hard look, and they immediately looked down. She knew they were hiding something, but if even Nana Pea wasn't throwing them under the bus, she would have to get to the bottom of it later. The four of them left the house and got into Dior's all-black Charger SRT Hellcat with all-red rims. And the girl hadn't just gotten the car for the look of it. She loved driving fast. The whole way to the mall, Nami found herself bracing in the front seat and questioning why she hadn't just driven her own car. When they arrived at Lenox Mall, Dior valet parked her car, and they went inside. It was Friday, so, of course, the mall was packed with people shopping and getting ready for the weekend. The first place Nami wanted to stop was the Louis Vuitton store, but as they walked and she stared in the distance, she saw something that made her think her eyes were playing tricks on her. A man stood in front of the Louis store, looking at his phone. There was something so familiar about his face and his stance, something so nostalgic, that she felt instantly drawn to him. Every time she tried to focus on his features, a passerby got in her way. She had to get closer.

"Me and Jah about to go to Neiman's real quick. Where y'all goin'?" she heard Zilla ask, but she had already separated from them.

She heard Dior calling her name from behind, but Nami's pace just quickened, trying to get closer to the person she had her sights on. Could it be? And then it happened. She finally caught up with him, and he looked up at her, stopping her in her tracks. She gasped as she stared into a set of eyes that mirrored her own on a handsome face she knew all too well. The jaw structure, the nose and the lips. He even stood like him.

"Rome?" she breathed.

Chapter 27

The tension in Cairo's car was so thick that it could be cut with a large knife. The silence was heavy. Neither he nor Toosie had said a word to each other after leaving their father's office. The truth was, Toosie didn't know what to say. What could he say? Of course, he wanted one day to move up the ranks and be trusted to meet their father's drug connect, the same way Cairo was. He just didn't want it the way it was given to him. He glanced over at his big brother and saw a look of concentration on his face. His jaw was clenched, and he was focused on the road in front of him.

"Cairo, I—"

"Unless you gon' tell me why the fuck you threw me under the bus like that, I don't wanna do no talkin' right now," Cairo cut him off dryly.

"How the fuck I throw you under the bus?"

"Tellin' Pop I started that shit."

"Dad asked what happened, and I just told him the truth. If you don't like that, then maybe you shouldn'ta did that shit," Toosie told him with a shrug. "I honestly thought he was gon' be madder than he was."

"He demoted me. What do you mean?"

"Is that so bad?" Toosie asked.

"Of course, you would say that. I forgot, you the one who got the job now. You always was his golden child."

"Me?" Toosie made a face. "Motherfucka, if I was that, then he woulda gave me the job in the first place. Not just 'cause you fucked up."

"He gave it to me because I'm the oldest. Shit, it's damn near my birthright. But now, I'm wonderin' if he always wanted you to take over. I can't believe this shit."

"You really can't see why he did what he did?" Toosie asked, and Cairo said nothing. Finally, Toosie let out a big breath. "Bro, you're crazy. You don't think; you just react. That shit is dangerous in business. You don't just put yourself at risk; you put me at risk, too. That shit *been* annoyin', and this time, ya shit done affected Dad. Maybe this step down is what you need to focus on gettin' ya mind right without the stress of such serious responsibilities."

"You Dr. Phil or somethin', motherfucka?" Cairo asked, a small smile coming to his lips.

"Nah," Toosie said and grinned. "And even though I'm in charge now, you ain't gotta worry about me bossin' you around."

"I wouldn't listen, no way. Promotion or demotion, I'll always be your *big* brother," Cairo side-eyed Toosie and shook his head. "I'll tell you everything you need to know about Rafael and his crew so you don't fuck up the transaction."

"Bet," Toosie nodded. "In the meantime, we need to go get that video footage from The Plaza. Maybe somebody around there know where we can find them twins that was shootin' at us."

"We can do all that, but first, I need to make a stop," Cairo said.

They'd been driving back toward where their condos were only five minutes apart in Buckhead when he suddenly decided to veer to the right and go toward Lenox Square. He drove all the way to the mall and parked in one of the parking garages. Although a shopping trip wasn't abnormal for them to embark on, Toosie felt there were more pressing matters at hand.

“Why we here?” Toosie asked, and Cairo pulled out a broken chain from his middle console.

“I need to get this fixed. Motherfucka cost me twenty thousand. I don’t even know how it got snatched off my neck last night.”

“Why not just wait for Marco?” Toosie said, speaking about their jeweler.

“He out of town for the weekend, and I want my shit fixed today. It’s a little spot in here that can do it. It won’t take long.”

He got out, and Toosie followed. When they were younger, their father used to want them to always walk with security. That was when they found out who Slaw was in the streets and what kind of past their father truly had. Normal young Black boys didn’t need three big, bulky dudes with guns escorting them everywhere. But when they got older, they didn’t feel that the security was protection. It made people more curious to know who they were. It was impossible just to be a fly on the wall. But Slaw didn’t care. He always wanted them safe. But when the two proved that they were more than capable of defending themselves by taking boxing classes and perfecting their aim, he eased up on them.

The two of them walked into the crowded mall, armed, even though there was a strict no-weapons policy. Toosie let Cairo lead the way, and he followed closely behind, his eyes jumping from person to person as he scanned his surroundings. As usual, the two of them attracted a lot of female attention as they walked. Toosie checked out some of the finest and thickest women he’d seen in the city. He loved a bad chick, but it took more than looking good to attract his attention. As a Libra man, he needed mental stimulation more than anything, and most of the women he’d encountered had the IQ of a snail. He found out that even the ones that seemed innocent would do anything for some money, and he meant *anything*. When they got to the jewelry store inside the mall, Cairo made to go inside, but Toosie kept walking.

"I'm about to see what Louis is hittin' on," he said.

"A'ight, I'll come find you when I'm done."

Toosie kept it pushing all the way to the Louis Vuitton store. Memories from the night before had already started to fade. Toosie was all about forward movement. The last time he could remember feeling sick for longer than a day about something that happened was probably the first time he helped dispose of a body. The man had crossed his father by taking a cut from the top of his father's money, so he had to go. Slaw had made Toosie cut off the man's ring finger so he could send it to his wife's home, the ring still on it. After that, death got easier for him to process. Because no matter when or how, everyone had to go some way and someday.

He went inside the Louis store, and, as always, the hushed reverence always struck him as absurd. A few attendants orbited him like well-dressed satellites immediately upon his entrance and offered their assistance. Their smiles were practiced, and their eyes were assessing him. He watched them scan him from head to toe before seemingly concluding that he was a man who liked the finer things in life. Toosie loathed pretension, but still, he let them take him to see their latest men's collections. He saw a silk shirt that caught his eye and took it off the rack.

"This one, what's the drape like after a few washes?" he asked out loud.

One of the attendants in the male section, a young, white man with a clean haircut, launched into a detailed explanation of thread count and weave. His words flowed like a well-rehearsed script. Toosie nodded, absorbing the information, but his eyes had already drifted to another shirt. He looked around for a bit longer and, in the end, ended up with three shirts and a few pairs of jeans.

"Your total is $22,000.15. Will that be cash or card?" the monotoned cashier said from behind the register.

"Card," Toosie said and handed her his card.

By the time he made it out of the store, he hoped Cairo would be done. He'd spent a good thirty minutes inside. Toosie stopped and stood rooted to one spot outside of Louis Vuitton, texting Cairo to see how much longer he'd be. As he looked down, the voices of all the loud shoppers blended like a hum. However, even with the noise around him, he could still sense someone walking up on him. He looked up and was suddenly staring into the face of a woman he'd never met before. She was much older than he, although the only tell of that was the streaks of grey in her hair and her mature presence. The thing that got him was her eyes. They were the exact same color as his.

"Rome?" she asked.

Toosie looked around to make sure she was talking to him. When he didn't see anyone standing near him, he looked back at her and pointed at himself.

"You talkin' to me?" he asked, and upon hearing his deep voice, her lower lip began to tremble. The expression she wore was one of wonder as her eyes jumped to every feature on his face. Suddenly, she seemed to lose her balance and almost fell, but Toosie caught her. "Whoa! You okay? You don't look good. Maybe you need to sit down. Here."

He guided her to a nearby bench, and the two sat down. He gave her a concerned look as she got herself together.

"I'm . . . I'm fine. Thank you," she said, seeing the worry on his face.

"It ain't no problem, ma'am. You here by yourself?"

"No. I'm here with my sons and my niece. We're up here shopping for me something to wear to my surprise party."

"Then how is it a surprise party?" Toosie asked, amused.

"My husband couldn't hide the left hand from the right from me if he tried. He's trying to do something sweet for me, but I don't want to go."

"To your own party? That's crazy."

"I just hate my birthday, that's all. Haven't celebrated in years."

"Why?"

"Years ago, on my twentieth, my brother was killed at my party. I just haven't cared to celebrate since."

"Damn . . . I'm sorry to hear that, ma'am. But you should still go, I'm sure ya brother wouldn't want you to be sad every year on account of him," Toosie told her.

"*Ma'am?* That makes me sound so old. Call me Nami," she chuckled as she stared into his face so intensely that Toosie almost started to fidget. "I'm sorry I approached you like that. You just look so familiar. What's your name?"

"Toosie, well, Tyri, but I go by Toosie. I was named after my dad."

"Oh, what about your mom? Maybe . . . Maybe I went to school with her."

"Draya, but she's a little older than you, though, so I don't know. Maybe you're thinkin' of somebody else."

"*D-Draya?*" She sucked in a swift breath, and her eyes widened slightly.

"Yeah, you know her?" Toosie's brow furrowed a little, wondering if the woman might have had an issue with his mom back in the day.

"No . . ." The woman quickly shook her head. "I must have been mistaken. This might be strange, but my birthday party is going to be at The Wiz Ballroom on Sunday at around seven. I have two sons around your age. You seem like the kind of young man I'd want them around. Maybe you can stop by and meet them?"

"Uhhh . . . I don't know. I think I'm a little too old to be making friends," Toosie said, and they both laughed.

Just then, he got a text message on his phone. He looked and saw it was from Cairo. It read:

I just saw them boys from last night. Meet me in the food court now–first level.

Toosie jumped to his feet immediately, startling the woman.

"Now, it's my turn to ask, are *you* okay?"

"I'm fine, I just have to go find my brother. Are you good? Do you need me to get you some water or somethin'?" he asked, and she smiled.

"I'm fine. But think about Sunday, okay?"

Toosie nodded and took off toward the food court. Nami seemed like a nice enough lady, but he had no plans on going to a stranger's birthday party. Not to mention that it was unusual for her to invite him at all. Maybe she was just a sweet woman, though. He weaved in and out of the crowd until he reached the food court and spotted his brother seated at a table near a Sushi bar.

"Where they at?" was Toosie's first question when he got to the table.

"Right there," Cairo pointed at something in the distance behind Toosie.

He turned, and sure enough, it was the twins from the night before. They were standing with a pretty young lady in front of a restaurant, waiting for their food. Toosie sat down next to Cairo and focused on it like a hawk.

"What we doin'?" he asked. "There are too many witnesses for us to get at 'em right now."

"I say we follow 'em and see where they goin' after this."

"Nah," Toosie shook his head. "We don't know where they parked, and even if we did, we would need to get to our whip to follow 'em."

"Fuck these people. Ain't a camera in here some money can't scrub clean," Cairo said, and Toosie saw his trigger finger twitch.

"That's stupid, and exactly the kind of thinkin' that got us here in the first place."

"Then what the fuck we gon' do? We can't just let 'em leave."

"I—" Toosie stopped immediately when he saw Nami, the woman he was just speaking with, approach the twins. One of them put his arm around her and kissed her forehead, and suddenly, he remembered that she said she was there with her sons and her niece. He almost couldn't believe his luck as a slow grin spread across his face. "We might not be able to follow 'em today, but I know exactly where they'll be Sunday at seven o'clock."

Chapter 28

Slaw sat at his mahogany desk, the leather of his high back chair creaking softly as he leaned forward. The door to his office was closed, but it did little to muffle the escalating shouts that echoed closer and closer.

"Where the fuck is he? Where is Slaw?" the familiar voice roared, punctuated by a string of curses.

Slaw had been expecting it, so his expression was impassive. Yet, there was a slight tightening of his jaw in preparation for the inevitable. He could hear the frantic tone of his secretary, Jan, trying to intercept the approaching storm. Her efforts were clearly failing, and the furious shouts only grew louder and closer.

"Here we go," Slaw murmured to himself.

He got up and went around his desk to face the approaching cyclone just as the office door ripped open with a violent crash. Jan, a middle-aged woman wearing a two-piece skirt suit, looked beyond flustered as she tried to hold Luther Williams back. She just wasn't a match for his six-foot, solid 200-something-pound stocky frame. Her golden skin seemed flushed as she looked at Slaw, her expression one of apology and fear. She knew that the only ones allowed back without permission were his sons, and even they had to knock. However, Slaw had been waiting for Luther to arrive and knew the man wasn't going to be happy when he did.

"I'm sorry, Mr. Wells. I tried to have him wait."

"No worries, Jan. Please go back to your desk and hold all my calls," Slaw instructed, and Jan gladly rushed out of the office, closing the door behind her.

Luther, dark skinned with a head of closely cropped greying hair, stood and glared at Slaw for a moment. He was a stark contrast to the polished elegance of the office. His expensive suit, tailored to perfection, couldn't mask the raw rage that radiated from him. His face was contorted with both fury and grief, his eyes burning with an intense and almost manic energy. Pointing a finger at Slaw, he jabbed it as he approached. His mouth sputtered, and his lips trembled, but no sound emerged. Veins throbbed in his temples, pulsing with the effort of trying to contain the uncontainable. Finally, when he was a few feet away from Slaw, he stopped. His finger dropped, and his hands clenched into fists.

"What . . . happened?" he said in an angry and shaky voice. "I sent my son here ahead of me so that we could wrap up the ACC deal. We were supposed to be celebrating a multimillion-dollar deal with the government of our country. So, tell me now why the fuck am I just now leaving the morgue? How did Lex die?"

Luther had angrily barged into his office, but Slaw allowed himself to feel empathy for his loss. He knew how he would feel if someone called him and said either of his sons had been murdered. He would not only barge into the office, but he would also have a gun down someone's throat. He knew Luther had three sons, but Lex had been the baby boy.

"He was shot last night while he was out with my sons on the town," Slaw said evenly, watching the different waves of emotions come over Luther.

"So *your* sons got *mine* killed?"

"There was an altercation that escalated. Lex drew his gun first, and I know y'all get down where y'all are from, but here, if you do that, you better have perfect aim. A shoot-out was had, and my sons were in just as much danger as yours. Unfortunately, Lex was killed on the scene," Slaw said.

"And he's the only one that died? What kinda security are they? Useless!"

"Security? Useless?" Slaw felt his empathy fade immediately. "Luther, I understand you're grieving. But my boys won't be blamed for the actions of the one who killed yours. What happened is a tragedy."

"A tragedy?" Luther asked, and his voice got louder. "A *tragedy?* My son is *dead!*"

"And I assure you that I have my boys out looking for whoever is responsible, because it easily could have been one of them. And that means whoever was shooting disrespected *me*. And I don't take kindly to that. You have my word that they'll be found, and they *will* pay." Slaw moved forward, put his hand on Luther's shoulder and looked sincerely into his eyes. "They'll pay with their lives."

"They better," Luther said forcefully, his nose flaring. "Or else we might as well start negotiating a buyout for Williams Enterprise. I know your share is bigger than mine, but over the years, I've become friends with some powerful people. People more powerful than even you, Slaw. Do you understand?"

His expression was so serious that Slaw almost believed him. They held each other's gaze for a few seconds before Slaw patted Luther on the shoulder. Then he stepped back and smiled grimly.

"I know when you look at me now, you see a polished man with many multimillion-dollar businesses. A lot to lose." Slaw's voice was so chilling that it felt like the temperature had dropped significantly in the room. "But, Luther, I don't take kindly to disrespect or threats. And

I assure you that you don't want to end up where the people who have done either end up. Or their families. Killing giants is what I'm good at. Do *you* understand *me*?"

It was then that Luther saw a flash of the true monster within Slaw. Although still very upset, he simmered down once he was reminded of exactly who was standing in front of him. He nodded slowly.

"I'm . . . I'm going to need some time to arrange for Lex's body to be shipped home and for his funeral. We may need to postpone the ACC meeting until then," he said.

"Take all the time you need to grieve, but Monday is the signing meeting. You need to be there. Chin up."

"But my son—"

"Is dead. And business must continue," Slaw said, turning his back on Luther and going to sit in his desk chair. "But in the meantime, whoever did this *will* answer for it. Now, I'm sure you have more important things to attend to."

The dismissal of Luther was subtle but conveyed effortlessly. Luther clenched his jaw and huffed out a puff of air before turning on his heels and marching out of the office. He was moving so fast he almost ran right into Slaw's wife as she opened the office door. However, she was able to get out of the way in time before she became roadkill. Her eyes darted from the furious look on Luther's face to the relaxed one on Slaw's.

"I take it that didn't go very well," Draya said once Luther was gone and closed the door before making her way to her husband's desk. Once there, she sat on his lap and wrapped her arms around his shoulders, then leaned in to kiss him softly on the lips. When she pulled back, she stared into his eyes. "What happened?"

"He threatened me," Slaw told her, and she raised a brow.

"And he walked out of here alive?"

"I gave him a pass. His son was just killed last night. If it was one of our boys, the whole city of Atlanta would be on fire by now. Plus, it's not him I'm worried about."

"Who is it you're worried about then?" she asked, studying his face.

"Cairo. If he wasn't so hotheaded, none of this would have happened."

The one thing that Slaw hadn't mentioned to Luther was that it was his own son who had started the fight in the first place. Cairo might have been the spitting image of Slaw, but he had yet to tame the monster inside of him. At his age, Slaw might have been consumed by the thirst for power, but there was a reason he was always the leader. He was always able to think clearly with a sound mind. Cairo acted first and thought no further. He felt it was a strength, but it was a weakness because it made him easy to read.

A stream of memories overcame Slaw, each one a jagged piece of glass gnawing away at his ego. There were so many signs that Cairo was spiraling out of control that Slaw chose to ignore. But the truth was the boy's temper had always been there. Just simmering under the surface like a dormant volcano. As a child, it was tantrums over toys or fights with Toosie about the most minor things, but that was easily dismissed. As a teenager, he began getting into fights and trouble at school, which Slaw chalked up to him trying to find his place on the food chain. But then, it never stopped. It just got worse, and now, it was getting in the way of business. Slaw couldn't have that.

"I told you we should have gotten him some counseling when that baby mama of yours dropped him off on our doorstep after we got married, especially when she got hooked on drugs. It probably traumatized him, and he never talked about it."

"I'm not going to let him blame his mommy issues for the fact that he's fucking with my money."

"What are you going to do?"

"I already did it. I demoted him," he told her, and her eyes widened.

"Baby, I know he fucked up, but you can't demote him. He's the only person who has ever met with Rafael other than you. And there's no way you can run all these businesses and take on that role again in the dope game too."

"I know, and that's why I promoted Toosie."

"Toosie?" she asked, and he heard the uncertainty in her voice.

"You don't think I should have done that?"

"Don't you think that might cause a wedge between them?"

"It might. Or it might bring them closer."

"What if Toosie isn't ready? Plus, I can't see Cairo taking this too well."

"Then it should push him to both do and be better. But then again, Toosie might be a natural at being the boss," Slaw said and felt his face grow serious. "His birth father was Rome, after all."

Chapter 29

"Zilla, Jah, come help me in here," Nana Pea shouted from the kitchen of The Wiz Ballroom.

Jyair had really put his all into planning his wife's forty-fifth birthday, and Nana Pea wanted everything to be perfect, especially the food spread. But try as she might, she just wasn't a spring chicken anymore and needed some help carrying everything. She waited a moment, but when neither of the twins popped up, she grabbed a tray of chicken and carried it out into the grand ballroom. It was not a short walk given the size of the place, but she enjoyed every sight she passed.

Light cascaded from massive crystal chandeliers, and their prisms scattered rainbows across the polished marble floor. The tall, arched windows offered clear, beautiful views of the manicured gardens surrounding the building. On top of that, Jyair had hired a professional decorator to come and tailor the decorations specifically to Nami. The tables, draped in layers of pink and white silk, were meticulously arranged throughout the vast space. Each had towering centerpieces of silver branches intertwined with delicate pink orchids and shimmering crystals. Silverware gleamed under the soft light, and crystal champagne flutes sparkled, ready to be filled with celebratory bubbles. Several balloon arches and towers of accenting colors filled in any arched windows. The photo backdrop was one of Nana Pea's favorite parts. She loved the large LED light marquee letters spelling out Nami's name beside it.

The food and dessert tables were almost complete. Just a few more heavy pans of meat left to bring out. Nana Pea looked around but didn't see anybody but the decorator applying finishing touches. Melo, Dru's longtime friend, and Jyair were reorganizing some of the tables while Dru and Dior had gone to pick up Nami. Both Jyair and Melo were dressed in formal attire. Melo's bald head seemed to reflect the ceiling light as she approached them.

"Jyair, where are those sons of yours? Guests are about to start showing up, and I need all this food out of the kitchen," Nana Pea said, throwing her hand on her hip.

"They're around here somewhere with Michael," Melo said, referring to his own son. "Knowin' them, they probably in a closet gettin' higher than a kite for the party."

"I wish they'd stop doin' that shit. You know Ro—"

"Didn't do drugs," Jyair and Melo finished her sentence for her, and Nana Pea rolled her eyes.

"Well, he didn't. He liked keeping his mind as sharp as he could."

"Trust us, Pea, we know there ain't never gon' be another Ro," Jyair said with a laugh. He looked around, still smiling. "It's crazy to think that the last time I saw him was twenty-five years ago. Shit still feel like yesterday. We all was s'posed to grow old together."

"Yeah, well, fate had other plans, baby. But because of Ro, we're all still together. How about that?" Nana Pea said, patting him on the cheek.

"You know, I don't think I tell you thank you enough for all that you do for the family. I don't know what we'd do without you," Jyair said, placing his hand over hers as it rested on his face.

"You tell me enough. And it's me who doesn't know what I'd do without you. What happened to Jelia was terrible. I couldn't even imagine leaving after that. And then when y'all had them badass babies, I, for sure, couldn't leave them. Zilla and Jah woulda tore you and Nami to the floor. And, whew, Dru just had to get that triflin' girl pregnant. Thank God Dior ain't nothing like her."

"Yeah . . . I know Ro is restin' at peace knowin' it's you watchin' over y'all grandbabies."

Nana Pea felt a warm rush of affection at the word "y'all." Flashes of Jelia dying in her arms suddenly came flooding back to her, and she found herself getting choked up. Jelia wasn't able to have any last words, and Nana Pea would never be able to forget watching the light in her eyes slowly dim. She would have loved her three grandchildren fiercely, and Nana Pea hated that they would never get a chance to meet her. But before she became a pool of tears, she snatched her hand away and made a shooing motion with it.

"Let me go find those damn boys. This is a party for their mama, not them."

She turned away just as a tear dropped, which she wiped quickly before walking out of the ballroom. That evening, she wore a long, flowing, light blue dress that gently brushed the ground as she walked. Making her way down the wide hallway to the tall front double door entrance of the ballroom, Nana Pea was preparing to go outside and see if the boys were in one of their cars. But as she passed a supply closet door, she heard the faint sound of laughter along with the smell of marijuana. She snatched open the door, and, sure enough, standing in the closet were Zilla, Jah and Mike Mike, passing a joint among them like they were on a regular street corner. All wore fitted suits and looked just like the younger versions of their fathers. Upon seeing her standing in the doorway, they suddenly looked like deer caught in headlights.

"I been calling y'all for thirty minutes straight," Nana Pea exaggerated and snatched the joint from Jah.

"Not the gas, Nana," Jah said in distress as she threw it on the ground, stomping it with her foot.

"I don't care how grown you are, you won't sully this moment for your mother smoking and smelling like weed!" Nana said sternly, then turned to Mike Mike. He was their height and had the deepest, slanted brown eyes she'd ever seen in her life. He had smooth, almond-colored skin, and although his mother was Japanese, he still had the hair of a whole Black person. The baby starter locs he had lay on his head like raisins as he stared at Nana Pea with guilt all over his face. "Mike Mike, you're supposed to be the one who keeps these hooligans on the straight and narrow."

"My bad, Nana," Mike Mike said, calling her what the twins called her. "They dragged me in here and forced me to do drugs."

"*What?*" Zilla and Jah said in unison.

"I don't care who did what! Take y'all motherfuckin' asses to the bathroom and freshen up. Put some cologne over that shit and bring your behinds to the kitchen," she ordered.

"Yes, ma'am," they said and quickly left the closet.

Nana Pea shut the closet door and went back to the kitchen. She checked the time. It was six thirty. Guests would start showing up any minute as they'd been instructed to arrive half an hour early. When the boys finally came into the kitchen, she directed them on what to take and where to put it. As they did, she sat back and watched the twins closely. Their eyes were low, but their body language exuded happy, childish vibes. Yes, they could be serious when business was involved, and they could both fight and shoot better than most. But when they first got into the street life, Nana Pea had to admit she was nervous. At their age, Rome had surpassed them in many ways. He was an owner, an employer and a true boss. The twins hadn't unlocked that door in their brains yet. They needed someone to keep them on track and grow them up if they were going to have anything real in life. They needed a leader.

Chapter 30

"Surprise!"

Nami had braced herself to be overwhelmed by the large crowd of people that were all around the room, standing by their seats. She thought she would want to run away and retreat to her bedroom. However, when she walked into the massive ballroom and saw how much work and time her husband had put into making her birthday memorable, she felt the most profound sense of gratitude. She'd been holding Dru and Dior's hands as they walked her inside, but she let them go and covered her mouth in joy. Tears sprang to her eyes when the crowd shouted upon her entrance, and even though she'd known about the party, she was genuinely shocked by the wave of emotions that suddenly hit her.

Nami's eyes fell on her fine husband as he walked up to her, looking good enough to eat. Every part of her body reacted to him. Her nose inhaled his cologne, her lips twitched, wanting his lips on hers, and her clit jumped, making her want to slide away from the party she'd just arrived at to get in a ten-minute quickie.

"Happy Birthday, baby," Jyair told her, handing her a large bouquet of pink roses.

"Jy . . . This is beautiful," she said, falling into his arms.

"I know you said you didn't want a party, but I couldn't let another year go by without me celebrating the day the love of my life came to this earth," he said, kissing her softly.

"I can't believe you did all this for me."

"What do you mean, 'all this,' woman? This isn't even a crumb in comparison to how much I love you. You deserve so much more. Especially lookin' this damn good. *Mm-mm-mm.*"

Jyair took in Nami's effortless beauty. Her long hair had been flat ironed and rested around her shoulders. She'd gotten her makeup professionally done and had decided on a sexy satin dress with a draped collar. His eyes fell on a chain around her neck, and he smiled.

"This is the first time I've seen you wear that in years."

Nami touched the N pendant on the chain that Rome had gifted her twenty-five years ago. After that night, she locked it up and hadn't worn it since. But after recent events, she felt compelled to wear it to her party as a homage to the past and a look toward a hopeful future. She kissed her husband again just as the DJ in the corner started to cut up on the turntables.

The large crowd began to dance, then lined up for food or headed to the open bar for a drink. Jyair took her hand and led her, Dru and Dior to the head table in the ballroom where her sons were already sitting. She set the flowers in her hands down on the table as they got up to give her hugs.

"Happy Birthday, Mama," Zilla said, hugging her and handing her a large stack of money. "You know I'm not good with gifts."

"I bet you know what to get all them bitches you be chasing after, though," Dior said, taking her seat at the table.

"Aye, a bitch be good with a bite to eat and an outfit, but my mama deserves the world," he replied and flicked her off.

He stepped aside so Jah could come forward. He gave his mother a hug and a kiss before handing her a small bag.

"Here you go, Mama. Happy Birthday," he said.

"Y'all didn't have to get me anything. You are the greatest gifts," Nami said; still, curiosity made her look into the bag.

"I still wanted to get you somethin' priceless," Jah said with a special glint in his eyes.

She reached in, expecting to pull out a small jewelry box, but instead pulled out a rectangular gift wrapped in pink tissue paper. She set the bag and money down beside her flowers and began unwrapping. When she finished, she realized she was staring at the back of a golden picture frame. Nothing could have prepared her for the picture inside when she flipped it over. She gasped as she stared down at her mother, Rome, Dru and her sitting around a Christmas tree. She remembered it as if it were yesterday. It was Christmas 1989. She was 9 years old and smiling like she'd just won the lottery. Which she kind of had, since her mother was able to get her the big dollhouse she wanted. Nami's little arm was linked with Dru's on her left while her head leaned to the right on Rome's shoulder. They were also smiling big because they'd just gotten the Sega Genesis game console. Their mother sat behind them, beaming like a proud mama, knowing she'd made her kids the happiest on the planet. Another set of tears found their way to her eyes as she took in the photo.

"How . . . How did you get this?" she asked softly.

"Pea had it," Jah told her. "It was in Uncle Rome's room when she had to clean it out."

"Thank you for this, baby. Thank you." She pulled Jah into another tight hug.

"Technically, that's Nana Pea's gift to you, ain't it?" Zilla said, jealousy dripping from his voice.

"Don't be mad at him 'cause you can't be thoughtful," Dior teased.

"One more word and that emerald green dress gon' have pink cake all over it," Zilla threatened.

They continued to bicker in the background like siblings, and Nami let Jah sit back down. She kissed the photo where Rome's face was and placed it gently on the table where she would be sitting. She glanced at the table to thank Nana Pea, but realized that she was nowhere to be found.

"Where's Pea?" she asked.

"Probably in the kitchen. I'll go get her," Jyair said.

"No, I'll go find her. I need to talk to her about something anyway," Nami said, stopping him. "I'll be right back."

She gave him another kiss before walking away from them and going toward the kitchen area of the ballroom. As she passed by many of her friends and family, they expressed their well-wishes for her birthday. Many gave her tight hugs and quick pecks on the cheek. By the time she got to the kitchen, she had inhaled at least thirty different perfumes and colognes. She pushed open the door and saw Nana Pea there, cutting a carrot cake to take to the dessert table.

"Now, why didn't y'all hire someone to do all this?" she said, her voice shocking Nana Pea.

"Oh my goodness," Nana Pea said when she saw Nami standing there. Her eyes lit up, and she dropped the knife, rushing to hug her. She pulled away and let her eyes brush over every part of Nami. "You just look stunning! And you dyed your hair."

"I wasn't showing up to my own party gray!"

"That ain't nothing but wisdom, baby," Nana Pea said. "Happy Birthday, honey. I'm sorry I missed the surprise part. I've been back here trying to make sure everyone has everything they need."

"Once again, reasons you should have hired somebody."

"Girl," Nana Pea waved her hands at Nami as if she'd said something foolish, "I already compromised by letting that husband of yours get food catered. I can feed my own damn family, I told him. But he insisted. Anyway, you go back out there and enjoy your party. I'll be out there in a second."

She went back to cutting the carrot cake, but Nami didn't budge. She stood there, feeling her heart pounding against her ribs. The words she needed to say were perched precariously on the tip of her tongue. Every time she tried, each syllable felt weighted. However, Toosie's face had haunted her sleep since she laid eyes on him. Nana Pea felt her presence still there and gave her a quick, curious glance.

"Did you need anything, baby?"

"Yeah," Nami heard herself say.

"Well then, spit it out. You're missing your own party."

Nami opened her mouth, the air catching in her throat and formed a silent plea.

"Pea, I'm about to ask you something, and I need you to tell me the truth."

"What is it?"

"You were the closest to him, so you'd have to know. They lived with you."

"Nami, you're talking in circles. Who lived with me?"

"Rome and Draya," Nami said, and Pea stopped cutting abruptly to look up into Nami's face.

"What are you trying to ask me?"

Nana Pea's expression was one of both dread and guilt, and Nami felt like there was a hand tightening around her heart. She felt like the air in her lungs couldn't escape, nor could she inhale any.

"I . . . I saw a boy at the mall the other day, and, Pea . . . He looked so much like my brother," Nami said as she watched Pea's eyes begin to glisten.

"Does he?" she breathed barely above a whisper, her hand going to her chest.

"I . . . I talked to him. I couldn't stop myself. I was so drawn to him. His name is Toosie, and I asked what his mother's name was."

"And what did he say?"

"He said her name is Draya." Nami couldn't stop the tears from streaming down her face or the sob that escaped her mouth. "So, I need you to tell me, did that bitch have my brother's child?"

Pea's lip trembled, and she shut her eyes tightly as she took a deep breath. When she opened them, the guilt was even heavier because, now, it was drenched in apology.

"I found out she was pregnant shortly before Rome died. She never told him, and she wasn't planning on keeping the baby. But the night that Rome and your mother died, she came and told me that she was keeping the baby. And since I was the only one who knew about him, she tried to kill me, but . . ."

"But what?"

"But your mother walked into the kitchen," Pea said, sniffling. "The bullet meant for me went into your mother."

"So, you mean to tell me the reason my mama got killed is that Draya didn't want anybody to know about the baby?"

"Yes. And, Nami, we wanted to tell you—"

"We? Please don't tell me Dru and Jyair knew about this?" Nami asked in horror, and Pea nodded.

"I'm so sorry, Nami. We just thought it was best."

"To not tell me about my brother's *child?*" Nami heard her shaky voice escalating.

"You took his death harder than any of us, Nami. There was no way we could tell you about a child we'd never have access to. It would just break your heart even more."

"He has our eyes, Pea, for crying out loud! He belongs to us," Nami said tearily. "Nobody, and I mean *nobody,* would be able to keep me from my family. And that's why I invited him here tonight. He thinks his father is somebody named Tyri, but I plan on telling him who he really is."

"*What?*" Pea's eyes flew open as wide as saucers. The fear was evident in her face. "You did *what,* Nami?"

"I invited my nephew to my birthday party. That shouldn't be a problem," Nami said smugly and tried to turn on her heels to leave.

Pea moved faster than she had in years to catch her. She grabbed Nami by the arm and turned her back around to face her. Nami saw the terrified look written on her face, and she couldn't understand why it was such a problem that he would come.

"Nami, you don't know what you've done. No, no, no. Where's Dru?" Pea released her and tried to walk past, but that time, Nami grabbed *her* arm.

"What are you talking about? What are you so afraid of?"

"The other night, Zilla and Jah got into it with Slaw's boys, and they ended up killing a boy. *That's* why Jyair has been wanting them to watch their backs until things die down. Think, Nami. Who did Draya run off with that night?"

"Slaw . . . but what does that have to do with Toosie?"

"You said Toosie thinks his real father is a man named Tyri, right?"

"Yeah . . ."

"That's Slaw's *real* name! Toosie thinks Slaw is his *father!*"

A slow dread overcame Nami as the words settled in. "Oh. My. God. My babies!"

She and Pea moved as fast as they could out of the kitchen and rushed across the floor toward the main family table. Zilla and Jah weren't there anymore. The only people at the table were Michael, Dior, Dru and Jyair, all eating. The two women turned in circles, scouring every moving and still body. Nami's sons were nowhere to be found. Seeing their panic, Dru and Jyair sprang to action.

"What's wrong, sis?" Dru asked, trying to get her to stop moving.

"Where are my boys? Where are Zilla and Jah?"

"They went outside to smoke because they said Pea snatched their joint earlier. What's wrong?"

"Oh no. Not again!" Nami screamed, pulling away from him and running out of the ballroom with Pea on her heels.

Chapter 31

The music coming from inside the ballroom was so loud that Zilla and Jah could hear it from where they were in the packed parking lot. They were leaning against a random car, passing a freshly rolled joint back and forth, facing the setting sun. Jah was texting someone on his phone, but Zilla's attention was on the sky. He took a long draw from the joint and felt the effects of the weed make him feel like he was literally floating.

"Damn, you gon' pass it?" Jah said with his hand out.

"Nah, keep textin' that bitch. You ain't worried about this gas," Zilla said, laughing, but he handed over the joint. "This shit crazy, man. Mama ain't celebrated a birthday our whole lives."

"I know. You see that ice on her neck?" Jah asked and whistled.

"Yeah. Pops said Uncle Ro gave it to her at her last party. That man was gettin' real cash—at our age too. That shit crazy to think about."

"What you mean? We make a lot of bread ourselves," Jah said, inhaling the joint.

"Not like that, though. Pops said Uncle Ro was really a millionaire at 25. Imagine if he was alive now. There wouldn't be a Slaw. My favorite story is how he beat him down with his bare hands." Zilla sighed. "I wish he woulda stayed to make sure he was dead, though. 'Cause now, we gotta deal with his pussy-ass offspring."

Unbeknownst to the twins, two figures had emerged from the shadows at the far end of the lot. Had they looked up, they would have easily seen the shadows. But their guards were down. The shadows moved with predatory grace, their footsteps muffled by the cracked asphalt. Jah had just passed the joint back to Zilla and was about to respond when the two figures with drawn guns were suddenly on them.

"What the fuck?" Jah said.

They'd been completely thrown off and rose from the car. The men in front of them had similar builds. One was slightly taller than the other, and they both wore masks. Zilla instantly noticed the one with his gun on Jah. He recognized his light brown eyes immediately.

"Wasn't even no point in even wearin' them masks. We know you them boys from The Plaza," he said calmly. "Do what you came to do."

Zilla stood like a soldier, unmoved by the gun pointed at his face. In fact, he took another draw of the joint between his fingers before flicking it to the side. His arrogance must have irritated the demon inside the man in front of him. Zilla heard the angry huff of air release from his nose under the mask and saw a spark of fury ignite in his eyes.

"You the one who disrespected me," the masked man said, roughly pressing the gun to Zilla's head.

"I bumped into you in a parking lot, and you wanted to act tough in front of all them bitches. How it feel to know that ego got ya mans killed?" Zilla asked.

Angrily, the man in front of Zilla raised his hand in an attempt to pistol-whip Zilla, but Zilla used that window of opportunity to grab his wrist and struck him with a left jab. Zilla then hit him on the inside of his elbow, forcing him to drop the gun. It all had taken place in a matter of seconds, and his light-eyed partner was shocked by the sudden strike, so much so that he took his eyes off Jah, who quickly moved out of the way of the gun and grabbed Light Eyes by the arm, forcing his hand to face the ground. Startled, Light Eyes pulled the trigger, sending a bullet into the pavement. Jah twisted his wrist and head-butted him, causing him drop his gun as well.

A brawl of power ensued as each party tried to go for one of the guns on the ground. Neither twin was strapped because it was their mother's party. The only thing that seemed to work in their favor was that their opponents weren't as skilled in hand-to-hand combat as the twins. However, Light Eyes was giving Jah a run for his money, but still, he was no match for the powerful blows Jah was landing. The thuds could be heard in the night air.

Zilla finally was able to knock the person he was fighting back long enough to grab the gun he'd dropped. By the time he regained his footing, Zilla had the firearm aimed, and his assailant was staring down the barrel of his own gun.

"No!" Light Eyes shouted and shoved Jah away from him as hard as he could.

He jumped in front of his partner right as Zilla tapped the trigger, letting off a bullet with a loud bang. The bullet didn't hit its intended target. Instead, it hit Light Eyes in the chest. He landed hard on the ground on his back, breathing raggedly from the gunshot wound. The other man looked down at him in disbelief, and as Zilla prepared to finish him off, he heard the sound of feet and frantic voices shouting.

"Zilla? Jah!" he heard his mother's voice calling over and over.

He took his eyes off the man to look over his shoulder. He heard his mom but couldn't see her in the sea of cars. He turned his attention back to his target in time to see him booking it across the pavement, running as fast as he could. Zilla ran after him and fired wild shots at him, but missed.

"Shit!" Zilla said to himself, realizing he'd gotten away.

Angrily, he walked back to Light Eyes, whose breathing was labored. His blood was spilling out into the parking lot, and Jah had removed his mask. He was looking up at Zilla, and even as he lost consciousness and pain washed over him, Light Eyes wore a defiant look.

"Y'all shoulda learned the lesson when ya man got blew down," Zilla said to him, aiming the gun at his head. "Time to go night-night."

Right as his finger pulled on the trigger, what felt like the force of a strong man pushed the gun to the side, sending the bullet into the pavement right next to Light Eyes's head. Zilla looked up and saw that it wasn't a man holding his wrist. It was his mother.

"No!" Nami screamed out of breath.

With her were Nana Pea, Uncle Dru and his father. He didn't understand the concern in their eyes as they looked down at the man dying on the ground. Jyair snatched the gun from him, and his uncle Dru dropped to the ground beside the dying man and applied pressure to his wound.

"Mama, Pop, what are you doing? He tried to kill us!"

"I know, but he don't know any better," Jyair said and looked at Uncle Dru. "He gon' make it?"

"He losin' a lot of blood. We gotta get him medical attention—*now*. Help me lift him."

Together, they picked him up off the ground and started toward Uncle Dru's precious new Mercedes. He had never even let Zilla or Jah eat a pack of Skittles in it, but there he was, about to let a stranger bleed in it. When his mother tried to follow them, Zilla grabbed her arm.

"Mama, what's goin' on?" he asked, and she whipped back around to face him, her expression a mixture of worry, fear and anger.

"Look at his eyes! Look!" She forced Zilla to look at the fluttering eyes of the man as he was carried away. "He's your family."

"W-what?" Zilla asked, confused.

"What do you mean by 'family'?" Jah asked in the same shocked tone.

"That's Rome's son," she said with tears rolling down her face. "You might've just killed your fucking cousin."

Epilogue

The moon hung high in the air as a strapping farmer made his nightly rounds with two big farm dogs at his heels. The air was thick with the earthy scent of hay and manure, a familiar comfort to him after a long day's work. As he walked, whistling one of his favorite songs, his boots crunched on the gravel path as he approached the chicken coop. He had a motley collection of Sussex hens clucking contentedly as they settled in for the night. He scattered a handful of grain and watched their beady eyes gleam in the night light.

Next, he checked on his goats, a boisterous bunch of Nubians and Alpines. He heard their playful bleating echoing across the field. When he reached them, they jostled for attention, eager for a scratch behind their ears. He obliged them, chuckling at their antics. One goat bullied the others out of the way, forcing the farmer to pet him.

"Now, Joey, you ain't the only one who want some attention," he chuckled again, but still gave the goat more attention than the others.

He made sure their high gate was locked well so they couldn't escape in the night before finally making his way over to his pigs. They were a rowdy group of Durocs, wallowing in the mud. He reached into his pocket and tossed some apples, watching as they greedily devoured the treats. Their snorts and grunts were a symphony of porcine contentment, letting him know that it was okay for him to go inside.

Satisfied that all was well, he turned and walked toward the farmhouse, a cozy, two-story structure with a wide porch and a chimney puffing out a trail of smoke. The closer he got to it, the more he could smell the delicious aroma of roasted chicken and mashed potatoes that filled the air. He was almost at the porch when he heard an engine humming and saw the vehicle turn up the gravel road and rumble to a stop in front of the farmhouse. He shielded his eyes, squinting at the car, but he couldn't make anything out until finally the lights cut off. The driver's door swung open, and a tall man around his age stepped out. Many things alarmed the farmer. The first was the look of distress etched on the man's face. The next was the fact that he was dressed in formal attire, but blood covered his pants and suit jacket. The farmer sighed as he looked into the face of the man.

"I told you never to come here. Not after everything," he said grimly.

"I didn't have a choice. There's an emergency."

"There ain't nothin' serious enough for you to show your face around here, Dru."

"There is one," Dru said.

"And what's that?"

"We need your blood," Dru said desperately.

"What for?"

"For your son, Rome! Brother . . . You have a son, and he needs your blood. Your AB-negative blood. He's dying."

To Be Continued . . .